HBA 7 KEF

MNL BCN

AIRPORTS

BLQ ZRH

MUC

Alvaro Camblor

7 Airports

© Alvaro Camblor 2024

ISBN: 978-1-923289-20-8 (Paperback)

 A catalogue record for this book is available from the National Library of Australia

Cover Design: Alvaro Camblor and Clark & Mackay

Format and Typeset: Alvaro Camblor and Clark & Mackay

Published by Alvaro Camblor and Clark & Mackay

Proudly printed in Australia by Clark & Mackay

ABOUT THE AUTHOR

Born in Leon, Spain (1972). Graduated in BS Electrical Engineering, University of Wisconsin-Platteville.

Engineering professional with 26 years of experience in Management and Food Manufacturing.

This book was written in 73 days while working two full-time jobs at my current company.

7Airports@gmail.com

To Sonja...

CONTENTS

KEFLAVIK, ICELAND

KEFLAVIK

N63 59.1   W022 36.3

Elev **171'**   Var **21°W**

BIKF (11-1) 28 SEP 90

JEPPESEN

*ATIS **111.2**	
KEFLAVIK Ground **121.9**	
Tower **118.3**	

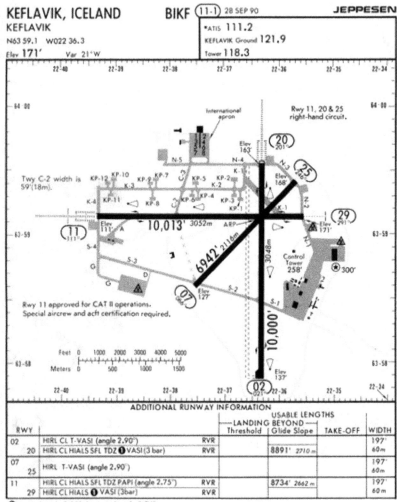

Twy C-2 width is 59'(18m).

International apron

Rwy 11, 20 & 25 right-hand circuit.

Elev 163'   (20) 201'

(25)

Elev 168'

N-5   N-4   N-3   N-2

KP-12 KP-10 KP-9 KP-7 KP-5 KP-2 K-1

K-3   K-2   N-1

K-4 KP-11   KP-8   KP-6 KP-4 KP-3 (29) 291'

Elev 171'

10,013' 3052m   ARP

6942' 2116m   3048m

Elev 111'   A   S-4

S-3

G   D

G   (07)   Elev 127'   S-2

Control Tower 258'   ✪300'

Rwy 11 approved for CAT II operations.
Special aircrew and acft certification required.

S-1

10,000'

Elev 137'

Feet 0   1000 2000 3000 4000 5000
Meters 0   500   1000   1500

(02) 021°

ADDITIONAL RUNWAY INFORMATION

RWY				USABLE LENGTHS			WIDTH
				— LANDING BEYOND —			
				Threshold	Glide Slope	TAKE-OFF	
02		HIRL CL T-VASI (angle 2.90°)	RVR				197'
	20	HIRL CL HIALS SFL TDZ ❶ VASI (3 bar)	RVR		8891' 2710 m		60 m
07		HIRL T-VASI (angle 2.90°)					197'
	25						60 m
11		HIRL CL HIALS SFL TDZ PAPI (angle 2.75°)	RVR		8734' 2662 m		197'
	29	HIRL CL HIALS ❶ VASI (3bar)	RVR				60 m

❶ Upwind angle 3.00° downwind angle 2.75°.

1

KEF

KEFLAVIK, ICELAND

"Sophie may be in Iceland. Go there. You will not find her in a five-star hotel. Check the hostels around the city and come back to me if you find something."

That was the handwritten note I got in my PO Box from my client, Alvin. I was not sure what made him think that I would find Sophie in Iceland. However, I am a professional solution provider. I don't question my clients; otherwise, I wouldn't have any. Although Alvin was my only client for the last year-and-a-half. He paid all my bills. At this point, Alvin was a full-time job for me.

I rented a car and drove 52 km to the capital, Reykjavik.

As I was driving through the empty streets, I thought to myself: "This city is full of hostels for backpackers...It is getting late, so better just pick one."

I ended up at the Circle Hostel, just by the sea and at a walking distance from the city centre. I checked in, and soon I realised I was not fitting there. It was full of young people visiting Iceland or making a stop between North America and Europe to save some dollars with the stopover.

I went into my room, just to realise it was a nine-person male dorm where I could have a small compartment for my luggage. Everything about me at that place was odd. My luggage, my clothes, my shoes, my age—but everyone was very respectful, and no one dared to make a comment. However, I know that in their minds, they must have been thinking that I had to be some kind of a divorced man trying to fix his first night out of his house.

It had been a long day already after the four-and-a-half-hour flight from Madrid, so I decided to go to bed early and save my strength for the following days.

A new day came up. A shower in the shared bathroom and a coffee in the communal kitchen were all that were available to start the day. As I sipped my coffee, I began drawing the plan in my head. I only wished Alvin was right and Sophie was staying in the city, and she had not gone for any outdoor activity.

Not sure if you have been to Iceland in November, but it is cold and the weather changes fast. I really didn't feel like freezing in the middle of a field, walking on a track, looking for Sophie.

I got myself a map and marked the plan on it for the day. I would start in the city centre, maybe with a museum and some standard local attractions.

I finished my coffee, brushed my teeth, and geared up to walk to the centre. It was sunny but chilly cold. As I walked, I was scanning everyone I crossed. Finding a blonde woman in Greece or Spain would have been less challenging. In Iceland? Any woman could be her.

My first stop was at the Iceland museum. Sophie had a soft spot for art and history. If Sophie was in Iceland, she would make a stop here. I walked through the rooms with one eye on the exposition and the other on anyone who could resemble her. Would she walk through the science hall, the art hall, the cultural hall, all of them? Impossible to know. After five hours in the museum, I was already exhausted. I sat in the middle of the souvenir shop and tried my luck, waiting for her to go through it if she were to leave the building. I waited until everyone was out, then I walked back to the hotel with the feeling of having wasted an entire day of work.

The second day in Iceland started like the first. This time, I decided to take a more touristic approach to the search and basically follow a group of Asians that were being guided through the city centre. They took me to Hallgrimskirkja, the cathedral of the city. It looked different from the other cathedrals in Italy, Germany, France or Spain. It was a modern-art cathedral. Straight lines, symmetrical and very clean and cold. I thought it was impressive with its 73-metre tower.

I stepped into the building and sat down, contemplating the vast space within the walls. I know Alvin was not paying me to contemplate spaces but to find Sophie and solve the case. I don't know, maybe at this point a little help, even if it were a divine inspiration, would be well received.

I hadn't had any breakthrough since I took the case a year-and-a-half ago. Alvin seemed to be a patient, methodical person, but I was not sure how much he would be able to take without any progress. In fact, Alvin had provided me with most of the clues, and I had just relied on them to carry on my job. So far, unsuccessfully.

Sitting there was not going to help, and the providence would not come to rescue me. I decided to take the elevator to the tower. I climbed the steps to the observation deck. The sights were impressive. On a sunny day, you could see the whole city, as well as the volcano on the other side of the bay. It really struck me that the church was not aligned with the streets below. It was offset by about 30 metres. For such a linear design, this was annoying to me, for whatever reason.

From the top of the tower, I saw a blonde woman leaving the cathedral alone. It was difficult to tell from 73 metres high if she would be Sophie. I rushed downstairs and into the elevator, trying to reach the street and not let my hunch fade away. I ran out of the cathedral and into the street that led to the harbour. I ran until I had her in sight and then slowed down to catch my breath. I followed her from a distance, waiting for her to give me a hint of her persona.

She walked into a small café next to the harbour. I thought it was comical that the name of the cafe was 'Cafe Haiti'. On a chilly day and so far north from the Caribbean, it was like light in the middle of the night.

As I was going to grab the handle of the door, an SMS arrived on my phone.

"I will be at Keflavik airport on 8 November. Departing on the Norwegian DY1718 flight at noon. Meet me there."

Darn! Alvin was coming in, and I was as lost as I was when I landed. No information, no clues, no hints, no Sophie, no nothing—I had nothing! This message basically gave me 32 hours to figure out something.

As soon as I got done calculating how much time I had left, I remembered that I had actually been following this blonde woman. So I really did have something. I opened the door and went into the cafe. It was quite crowded. All tables were full, and more people were queuing to order either food or coffee. I looked around. I couldn't find her. Maybe she was there, but with 90 per cent of the population being blonde, "Hell, who knows!"

There was a door on the other side of the cafe. She could have just left through that door. There were too many people in the cafe for me to try to get through them. I was not going to create by panic going through the cafe like a maniac. My only option was to run to the other side of the building. By the time I walked the distance, there was no one to be found. It was already too dark to see anyone. It was five o'clock, and in these latitudes, at that time of the year, it meant it was already fully dark. Iceland is not Belgium, where all the streets have lights. Here, this was the absolute minimum they could go by.

It was late and cold, and a freezing drizzle had just begun. I walked back to the hostel.

I went to the shared kitchen and prepared something warm to eat. I sat quietly in the communal living room. I didn't have too much to share with all these young people. I was just mentally going through the case, trying to make sense of it.

"What are you doing here, man?" One of the young men asked. Come on, look at you. You should be in a five-star hotel, well, maybe at a four or three at least."

It took me half a minute to react. I was not even sure what kind of answer I could give. Should I tell the truth, or should I go for the kicked out of the house, husband story?

"I'm looking for someone."

"In Reykjavik? In a hostel? In this hostel? This is a stopover. No one stays here for more than three or four days. Only the locals and even the locals would go somewhere else if they could. Probably somewhere warmer. If that person were ever here, he or she is already gone."

"She."

"Ah, now this gets more interesting. Tell me all about it."

"I'm not going to tell you anything about it. It is none of your business."

"Ah come on, at least give me her name, maybe I know her."

"Sophie."

"Sophie? Sophie, nah, it doesn't ring a bell."

I kept quiet trying to avoid a conversation, but I had 30 hours left before Alvin would arrive. I was desperate, so I thought a couple questions would not hurt me.

"Eh, man, where all do you people visit when you are here?"

"There are a lot of cool places to visit."

"Give me some, be specific."

"The Iceland museum, the cathedral, the—"

"Been there already, where else?"

"The Iceland Punk Museum, the Icelandic Phallological Museum, Reykjavík Art Museum Hafnarhús, The HARPA Concert Hall, there are a lot of places to go."

"Really? A Phallological museum? You gotta be kidding me, right?"

"No, really, I was there today. It is full of, well, you know, 'dicks'."

"Any place that you would go to at night? Where do you go after dark?"

"Yeah, there are a couple of places where I have been recommended to go. What are you looking for? Women, weed, both, something else?"

"Where would a normal person go?"

"Any pub in Laugavegur Street. Try the Lebowski. It is quite popular, but I am not going with you, no way. You are on your own for that."

"Right. What can I expect over there?"

"Normal people having a drink, chatting and dancing."

"Right, thanks."

I finished my dinner and went to grab my coat. It would be a long walk on a chilly night.

The Lebowski seemed to be a nice place. However, it was almost empty. I sat at the bar and got myself a beer. To tell the truth, I felt more like getting a coffee or a warm soup, but I needed to maintain the appearance. Slowly, the venue began to fill. Some people sat at the tables, some at the bar. Music sounded louder and louder with time as if it was trying to make conversations among people more difficult. I guess, for the people dancing, it was needed.

I remembered that Alvin said Sophie liked to dance. I hated it. I have absolutely no rhythm whatsoever. I like to listen to music, but my body just can't find the coordination to dance. Yet, I found the courage to get off my stool and walk to the dance floor while holding a beer in my hand like a professional. I was not dancing. I was just making my way through, from one side to another as if I was trying to get somewhere, while I was scanning every face in the process. I did it a couple of times, but then I thought people were getting annoyed by me interrupting their fun. So, I went back to the bar and sat again.

I heard someone trying to talk to me, but at this point, the music was so loud that trying to understand the words in another language and with the Icelandic accent was of no use.

"What?!" I exclaimed.

"I'm Eli!"

"Who?!"

"Eli! My name is Eli!"

"Hi!"

At this point, the music changed to a slower pace and somehow to a quieter volume.

"Where are you from? You are not from Iceland, are you?"

"No, I'm not. I'm just here for a couple of days. You know, a stopover."

She looked at me somewhere between disappointment and disbelief. Disappointed, as only for a couple of days meant not a chance for any long-term proposals, and in disbelief as I didn't match the profile for a 20-year-old stopover sort of guy.

"Oh, I see. Well, never mind."

As she was turning away, I said,

"Hey, wait up! Let me buy you a drink. Relax! Just talk."

She thought for a second, looked at me and softly whispered, "Alright. I guess."

"What will you have?"

"...I'll get an 'Ölgerðin Þó'."

"Uh, you are going to have to ask that yourself. I can't even pronounce that. Get me a 'Lite'. I'll take the bill."

She smiled back and asked for the drinks as I reached for my wallet.

"Cheers."

"Skál."

"So, what are you doing in Reykjavik?"

I didn't feel like explaining the whole story again, so I cut it short.

"I'm looking for Sophie."

"No mocking around, eh? Well, I'm just Eli. Sorry. I know a couple of Sophies, maybe three or four, but unless you are looking for married women with kids, I don't think any of them are the ones you are looking for."

"Apologies, Eli. I didn't mean to be rude. I have explained the same thing too many times, and I just didn't feel like doing it again. But, yes, I am looking for this person on behalf of a client."

"Ah, a private investigator? That is interesting. I thought that was only in the books. Now you have caught my attention. Tell me more about your work. It is ok if you don't want to talk about your case. At the end of the day, it is just talking about work, right? And no one wants to talk about work after work! Just your profession. I have never met one."

"Well, sorry to disappoint you again, Eli. I am not a private investigator as you know from movies or books. In reality, I am an engineer, and I am trying to help someone with a problem. Let's say that's what the engineers do, right? There is a problem, and we try to figure out a solution. Sometimes, we solve how to go around or through a mountain, sometimes, we solve how to land on Mars and sometimes, we are asked to solve other things. For me right now, it is another thing. Not a real engineering problem."

"Interesting. So, how do you do it?"

"I approach it the same way as I would a real engineering problem. Data, analysis, logic, method…"

"Does it work?"

"Nah, not this time. I cannot make any sense out of this problem. I cannot find the logic, and the data is all over the place. It is not normal data, meaning, it is difficult to find a pattern. I'm getting a little bit desperate at this point."

"I see. Do you get any money for this, or is it a kind of favour you are giving or returning?"

"I get paid. Not that I will end up rich with this, but it pays the bills, and I travel a bit. I got to come to Iceland…In November!"

She laughed out loud.

"Yeah, right! Everybody's dream, coming to Iceland in November, when it is already cold and dark. Most people try to get away to a warmer place if they can afford it."

"And you?"

"I can't afford it! I mean, not that I don't have the money to do it, but I just can't."

"So, what do you do, Eli?"

I'm a kindergarten teacher. No holidays for me in November."

"Married? I'm sorry, I should not have asked."

"It is ok, divorced. It happens, but it is ok. We are civilised people. It didn't work, we split, we didn't make a drama out of it. No regrets, no hard feelings. This is a small place to make enemies for life."

"Kids?"

"Yes, one daughter. She is still too young, but she'll be alright. Half of the married people in Iceland get divorced. She will never feel odd."

"Care for another drink?"

"Ok, but this is the last one for tonight. I can't show up with a hangover in front of the kids."

"Deal. Can you ask again for the drinks?"

"Yes, but this time they are on me."

"Okie."

Eli asked for the drinks, and we continued our chit-chat until the lights of the bar blinked, signalling that it was time to close. She booked a ride back home. As we were waiting outside, she asked,

"Do you want to share it? It is late and cold."

"Nah, it will be alright, I'll walk."

"Thanks, it was a fun time. I enjoyed it."

"Me too."

"When are you leaving?"

"Not sure, in a couple of days I guess, you know, just a stopover."

She smiled as she wrote on a piece of paper.

"Here is my number. Will you call?"

"No, I won't, but I'll keep it for my next visit."

"It is ok. You seem to be a good guy. I hope you have a breakthrough in your search."

The ride arrived. I opened the back door for her. She gave me a hug, as if she had known me for years and got in the car. As I was going to close the door, she stopped it with her hand.

"Go to the Art Museum tomorrow. Maybe you will find Sophie there. If not, there is a tree, like a Christmas tree. Visitors can write messages on a piece of paper, and they can hang them on the tree branches as if they were Christmas decorations. Maybe she was there and left a note. Read them. If it doesn't work, you can leave her a message there. Maybe she will read it one day."

"I will, thank you. Please take care."

"I will, bye!"

With that, I closed the door and saw the car disappear into the darkness of the street. I walked back to the hostel. For the first time in a long time, I was not thinking about Sophie or anybody else, but about Eli. She really was such a nice person to talk to. I felt really bad telling her I would not call her back, but it wouldn't be fair. However, maybe, one of my biggest failures as a person has always been assuming people's behaviours, interests, reactions and outcomes. Making assumptions about people instead of letting them be and waiting to learn from them. Maybe in this case, the fair thing was to call Eli back, but I never did. I never saw her again.

Yes, that's a big flaw to have. A bigger one when you know about your flaw, and you neither can help it nor control it. And with that thought, I closed my eyes in my bunk.

The third day in Reykjavik began with the pressure of knowing that I had less than 30 hours before meeting Alvin. I left the hostel early and walked to the Art Museum, as Eli had suggested. Too early, I thought, as it was not closed yet. I walked around the block, trying to make some time until opening hour. The time came, and the museum opened.

I began visiting the different rooms. The first one on the top level was about Japanese art. It was a white room. Everything was meticulously spaced apart. I got as close as I could, and I figured out that it would be approximately 17 cm. What an odd distance to choose. Not 20, not 15. It didn't even fit in inches, and yes, I did calculate that as well. It was a mix of pictures, drawings and Japanese characters. Not a single theme or topic. Some in black and white, some in colour. All in the same white frame. All in the same size. From corner to corner of the wall. From the ceiling to the ground.

I moved into the next space. In one of the corners, there was a small table with a green lamp and an old rotary-dial telephone. I was not sure if that was part of the exhibition or just some type of legacy equipment from the old days of the museum. As I got closer, I saw the small label on the wall that eventually would clear my doubts.

An old woman came behind me and pointed at me.

"That is Yoko Ono's phone."

I turned around and looked at her, lost.

"You know who Yoko Ono is, right?"

"Hello. Good morning. Yes, I know who Yoko Ono is. She was John Lennon's partner, right?"

"That is correct. Hello, my name is Anne, and I work as a custodian at the museum. This is Yoko Ono's phone.""I don't understand. Did she own it? Did she design it?"

"Sometimes, she, Yoko Ono, actually will call this phone and have a conversation with whoever picks it up. Obviously, she doesn't call every day, not every month, not every year."

"…but, has she ever called?"

"Yes, she has. I heard the telephone ring and someone having a conversation with her. Well, only what the man was saying because I could not listen to her."

"…but why? I don't understand."

"Turn around."

I turned around and saw a wall full of photographs with some stories below. I walked the room and noticed that all of them were photographs of women's eyes and that there was some story below. Now, I was extra curious. I approached the wall and read the note from the artist,

A MESSAGE FROM YOKO ONO:

A call.

Women of all ages, from all the countries of the world:

You are invited to send a testament to the harm done to you for being a woman.

Write your testament in your own language, in your own words, and however openly you wish.

You may sign your first name if you wish, but do not give your full name.

Send a photograph of your eyes. The 'Testaments of Harm' photographs of your eyes will be exhibited in my installation from October 7th, 2016–February 5th, 2017, at Reykjavík Art Museum.

I started looking into the eyes of the women and reading the stories behind them. The stories were sad. Really sad. Most of them related to males abusing women and hurting them. No excuse is valid. Most of the stories of harm came out of tradition, religion, power, war and social status. No one is valid. And acknowledging that all the stories were terrible, the stories that pinched me the most were the ones where the harm done came out of love stories. Broken hearts, broken eyes, broken souls. How come love ends in hurt? When does it go wrong?

There is an old saying in Spanish that goes like this:"Whoever loves you well will make you cry."

I know there are many ways to read this, but love and crying just don't belong in the same sentence if you understand crying as crying out of sadness or pain.

I was now standing in the middle of the room while people walked around me. Just dwelling on my own thoughts.

I had spent two hours in that room, reading the stories and thinking about them. I had been so absorbed in the displays of eyes and pictures that I had forgotten about Sophie, or had I?

Every pair of eyes I looked at, I was looking for her eyes. Every love story I read, I was looking for a story that maybe could relate to her. Sophie was always at the back of my mind. Like an unresolved puzzle. A puzzle I had to resolve for Alvin, or at least get the information that would lead to her.

There was one more thing for me to do in the museum. I had yet to find the tree that Eli had mentioned. I walked the aisles until I found it. Eli was right. It looked like a Christmas tree with colourful notes hanging from the branches. Eli had very accurately described it. The tree was as I had pictured it in my head when Eli described it.

I got closer to the tree, and I began reading the notes. At least the ones that I could read. A lot of the notes were written in different languages, which I could not understand. Icelandic, German, Arabic, and some other languages that used symbols.

Some of the notes were signed. Some of them were not. I looked at all of them. Searching for a signature from Sophie or a note that could be from her. I was not able to find anything relevant. So, I decided to take Eli's advice and left a note on it. Who knows, maybe she would read it. I looked around, and I found a pen and paper already prepared for people to leave messages. I got my piece of paper and the pen, like I would know what the message would be. I didn't know what to write. I thought about a long explanation note. After a couple of minutes, I was just able to write,

Sophie,

I wish you were here.

17/11/2016

I didn't even sign it. I didn't provide a phone number or an email address. That was the only thing that came to my mind. I folded the piece of paper and placed it in a position that would stand somehow among the rest, with the idea that maybe Sophie would read it. However, my faith was diminishing by the minute, and even if she were to read it, she wouldn't be able to make sense out of it. But sometimes I do things that only have meaning to me. Not particularly useful, I guess.

I thought I had exhausted the possibility of finding Sophie or any clue about her in the museum. So, I decided it was time to move. I crossed the street and walked to the HARPA, which was a massive and impressive modern building for arts and entertainment. I was able to get into the building, but there was some kind of private event going on, and I could only enter the entrance hall and the bar area. I could have stayed in that building for hours, studying its engineering and analysing every bolt and nut on it.

Suddenly, I recalled the little, where I had followed the blonde girl from the Hallgrimskirkja cathedral the day before. I headed in that direction and decided to have something to eat and wait for Sophie to suddenly walk through the door.

I ordered some local food and a coffee and sat in a corner where I could watch both doors. I took out my notebook and pen and began drawing a diagram of this whole case. What I knew, what I didn't, the leads, the clues and the places.

Using my engineering training, I drew fishbone diagrams, flowcharts, matrices, random words and played Connect with them. Darn! I even tried to plot variables into a graph, trying to look for correlations. How do you get values to plot a graph when your variables are feelings and sensations? Still, nothing seemed to make too much sense. I just couldn't figure this one out.

People came into the cafe, stayed and went. None of them were Sophie. I sighed and went back to the hostel and packed my things. I had a feeling that Alvin would ask me to go back and look somewhere else.

The last day in Iceland was cold and rainy again. I went to the front desk, paid my bill and drove to Keflavik.

Sharp as a flight can be, there was Alvin sitting at one of the cafes with a cup in his hand and looking lost somewhere, in some other place, most probably thinking about Sophie. Alvin was always travelling. I was not sure where he was coming from this time.

I really didn't feel like talking to him. I didn't have too much to say. No progress in the case, no clues, no Sophie. I was not looking forward to this, but it had to be done.

"Hi, Alvin."

"Oh, hi. You are just in time."

"I know you hate people being late."

"You know me well. Tell me. Have you found Sophie?"

"No, I haven't. Neither do I have any clues on the case. I have been looking around, asking questions, leaving messages."

"Stop. It is ok. I knew you would not find Sophie here, but I thought maybe it would bring you some light into all this searching. I have decided that we need to put an end to this. Sophie is gone. For better or worse. She is gone. We will never find her. I don't even know if it even makes sense to search. Even if I found her, I am not sure what would be next."

"Ok, yes, I get it. So now what?"

He handed an air ticket across the table.

"Here is your ticket. Go back to your normal day-to-day. Your work, your friends, whatever you have. The case is over. You are dismissed. Free. Go."

I had known Alvin for the longest time. I knew his way of thinking and how he reacted to life. I knew he would never let this go in one way or another. Whatever the story was behind Sophie, it would haunt him forever.

"You know, I never asked questions. You gave me the information you thought was needed for me to do my job and that was enough for me. I tried to do my job as well as I could. Obviously, not too well, but sometimes people just lose. Sometimes we just cannot get our way. Sometimes it is our fault, sometimes it is not. Sometimes, it just happens. I am fine. The case is over. But look, we have two more hours of waiting before flying out. Why don't you tell me the story of Sophie? It would be good for me to understand that I have not wasted a year-and-a-half of my life chasing the wrong thing."

"You haven't. Sophie was the right thing and the right case for you to work on. Don't you ever think differently about that?"

"Ok, fine, then tell me, what is all this about?"

Alvin looked down at his watch, then looked up at the departure display. Closed his eyes, sighed, looked down and said,

"Ok, it is ok. I'll tell you the full story."

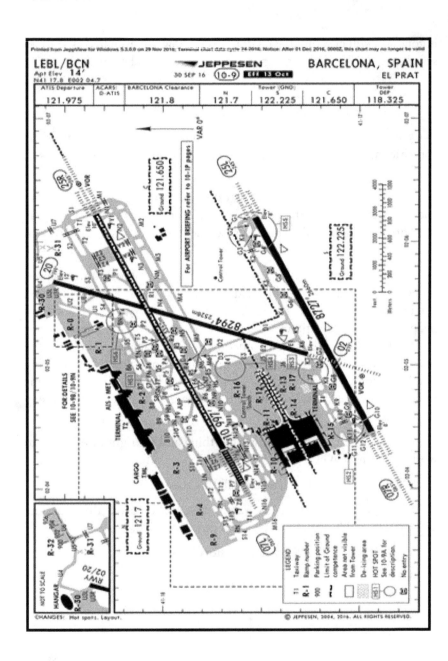

LEBL/BCN
Apt Elev 14'
N41 17.8 E002 04.7
JEPPESEN
30 SEP 16 (10-9) EFF 13 Oct
BARCELONA, SPAIN
EL PRAT

Printed from JeppView for Windows 5.3.0.0 on 29 Nov 2016; Terminal chart data cycle 24-2016; Notice: After 01 Dec 2016, 0000Z, this chart may no longer be valid

ATIS Departure	ACARS: D-ATIS	BARCELONA Clearance	Tower (GND):			Tower
			N	S	C	DEP
121.975		121.8	121.7	122.225	121.650	118.325

CHANGES: Hot spots. Layout.

BCN

BARCELONA, SPAIN

❝It was back in August 2013. I had been working three roles at the same time for the past year, and I really needed a change. Move cities, do something different. See different people. Travel a bit. Fly. Drive. Be nowhere. Spend time on my own. Talk as little as possible and think. That's what I really wanted to do. I was tired of the day-to-day. Working as a project engineer would give me a sense of living in the future where no one else is. When you work on a project or a new development, you always think about what will come and not about what has already happened.

Anyway, the company offered me to move cities and get a new job as an engineer, so I took it.

Pretty soon after I started the job, I was sent to a meeting in the south of Germany. However, in reality, I was not supposed to go to that meeting. That was not my project. Some German engineer had to work on it, but for whatever reason, he could not make it, and I was sent.

Sophie was fairly new to her company. I think she had been working there for less than a year. In any case, she was also sent to that meeting, but guess what? That wasn't her project either. She was not supposed to be there.

Sophie and I were never supposed to meet each other. Or maybe we were, but what were the chances? I still remember what she was wearing and how quiet she was. And her first words.

"Hello, I am Alvin, pleased to meet you."

"Hello, Sophie, good to know you."

We shook hands. All very formal.

The sense of touch is something I always try to remember. I always have had a very defined personal space. As a kid and then as an adult. Touching things is something I remember. A handshake only lasts for a few seconds. Two to four seconds, if you think about it. There is not much time to analyse or get feelings, but I usually get a feeling. Is it soft, hard, swallow, sweaty, crack, hairy, cold, warm, strong, kind?

I shook Sophie's hand, but I can't remember the feeling. I just can't and trust me, I have tried throughout the years to get that feeling back, those two, four seconds, with no success. I never touched her hand again until almost two years later, sitting in an airport bar.

Anyway, that is how I met Sophie.

The meeting came and went like any other meeting. Another work meeting. Nothing special about it. Nothing special about her. Yet.

We started to work on the project. At the beginning, Sophie was like any other colleague I had worked with. Same treatment. Same conversations. However, the relationship between the two of us evolved as the project was evolving. Except that the project was planned. What began to grow between the two of us was not. That was not planned. At least on my side, but I don't think it was on her side either. I think the day-to-day of the project just brought the both of us closer. You know, the meetings, the trips, the trials. We were always very professional about it. I mean, sometimes, we travelled together, drove around together and had food together. As I said, nothing different from other people I had worked with in the past.

A month before the project was due, Sophie told me that she would be quitting her job after the installation and commissioning were delivered. That caught me off guard. To some extent. It is not unusual for people to stop for a while after a long project.

I have never taken a break in all my years. It has been always one thing after another. Not that I am a workaholic or anything like that. I think it has been more of a need for me to keep going. Not to stop and think about decisions, a way to avoid my own life.

It seemed like the blink of an eye, but that project took 19 months to materialise. Which is just about the standard time for a project of that size.

Looking back at those 19 months, those were the best 19 months of my career. I never worked so hard, and I never enjoyed it that much. I worked as hard again, but I never enjoyed it like that. Actually, I never enjoyed working again.

Anyway, the project was delivered. Everything worked as expected. At least, from the engineering point of view, commercially that was another story. We both were good at our work.

The project was over, and Sophie made good on her word about leaving after the first successful production. We met at the head office. I hugged her tightly. Just a bit longer than usual. She said she would keep my contact and then she was gone. And with that, my void was formed.

The first week, I thought it would be just for a while, and the void would close on its own. Nothing to do. Just a little bit of time and that would be it. I have never been so wrong in my entire life, and the list of mistakes and errors in my life is long. Trust me.

I went back to my day-to-day. I was assigned another project, and I began working on it. Always professional but heartless somehow.

Sophie would sporadically contact here and there. She was always travelling. Various places and countries. She really seemed to be all over the place.

Months went by in this way. Me working, she travelling. Until the day she sent me a message suggesting the two of us meet in Barcelona.

Barcelona was one of the ten cities I would normally travel to for work. I was sure that I could make it work somehow. There was always a supplier to visit over there or a meeting to attend in the hub.

We agreed to meet at the end of the fall. Barcelona is a Mediterranean city—the weather would still be good. I flew into BCN a couple of days before Sophie arrived, so I could take care of the company business and be free to meet her. I rented a car at the airport, and I went to the usual hotel on the other side of the city.

I met some suppliers and listened to them, while they tried to sell me their equipment. Not paying too much attention and basically waiting for time to go by until I meet Sophie.

Wednesday, I woke up with a message from Sophie.

"I am arriving today. Let's meet at 17:00."

We agreed to meet at the Olympic Port. I like to be close to the ocean, or the sea, or a lake, or a river—close to the water. The waves crashing or the river flowing brings me a sense of peace like no other. For some people, being on top of a mountain brings peace. For me, it is being close to the water.

I arrived early at our meeting point. I always do. I hate it when people are late, and for me to be late somehow creates anxiety. An anxiety that I can avoid if I go early, so that's what I do.

"Hello, Alvin."

"Hello, Sophie."

We hugged. Longer than normal. Again, for me, it is all about time. You hug a friend. But no one thinks about how long it will take. I do. I feel it. I like hugs. More, when they last more than the standard friend or family hug. I feel it. With a hug, you give up your personal space. I think a hug is the most intimate show of affection you can have while still wearing clothes. Sophie broke the hug, looked at me and said,

"Should we go for a walk? I have been driving all day. I don't feel like sitting."

"Ah, yes, sure. Let's walk. How have you been?"

With that, we began walking. We walked at an easy pace. There was no hurry. I don't think either of us wanted to end the walk soon. The weather was nice, and the sunset was a beautiful orange-red one. She was telling me all about her trips. The places she had been, the people she had met. All the stories. The good, the bad, the ugly ones. Some of them she had already mentioned when she those sent messages. Others were new to me. She always tried to balance the conversation and ask questions to me. However, I didn't have much to say beyond work. In any case, I have never been a good storyteller. I'm normally a quiet person who loves to hear other people's story when they are interesting.

Sophie's stories were always interesting to me. She knew I would never interrupt her while she was talking, so it was always funny to me how she would take some pauses to allow me to enquire about the story. Often, I would just say, "Please, continue," and she would just smile and do so.

Her stories always had the right amount of information. She would give you enough details to picture the whole situation, but she wouldn't get into too many that would compromise your attention or make you lose track of the story.

We kept walking until the sun went down, and I suggested having a light dinner and heading back earlier.

"What do you feel like having for dinner, Sophie?"

"A salad would be ok."

"Alright, let's take this table by the seafront and order something."

We ordered our food and silence was established at the table.

"Tell me. How have you been?"

"I have been ok. Nothing special has happened around me. Mostly work."

"Ok, tell me about work then."

"Well, yeah. After our project, I got assigned another one, as you might expect. This one is more of a research and development kind of project."

"But you are not doing research and development. You are doing engineering, aren't you?"

"Yes, I am. They have a problem with one of the products, and the company just doesn't know how to solve it, so they asked me to investigate new technologies and innovate ideas."

"And have you?"

"Of course, I have! Have some faith in me, Sophie!"

"I do! I have always had faith in you. You always come up with something to solve the situation. Do you remember, during our project when everyone began panicking about the sealing and you just stayed cool and found a solution? For you, it is just a game, isn't it?"

"To some extent. It is only a job. There are more serious and important things in life. So, I tried to get the drama out of it, but in the end, the job needs to get done because it pays the bills. If I had to do it, I would rather enjoy it. And not just me, everyone around."

"Yes, that is so true. Tell me, who are you working with now? Anyone I know?"

"No one. I have been on this project alone. It is better this way. It is almost done anyway. I'll have to present it at the beginning of the year, but I don't think it will fly."

"Why is that?"

"I don't believe they will pay the price for it, but trust me, if they don't, they will pay it later with more losses."

"I'm sure they will."

Sophie was smiling. She seemed relaxed, comfortable, safe, but also tired. I decided to call it a night.

"I think it is time to go back to the hotel. Are you still ok for the trip to the mountains tomorrow?"

"Yes, for sure. Will you drive me back to my hotel?"

"Of course, I will."

I drove the car. We were silent. She was just looking outside the window, seeing the city go by. We arrived at her hotel. I stopped the car, and she gave me another hug. It is always difficult to give a hug in a car when wearing seatbelts, but we wouldn't finish the night without one."

"See you tomorrow? Nine, sharp?"

"Sharp! Good night, Sophie."

"Good night, Alvin."

I didn't go back to my hotel. I went to the beach. I parked the car and walked to the sea. I sat down right where the waves broke. I stayed there for a long time. Trying to think about not thinking about anything. I wanted to clear my mind. I tried to empty my head, but I couldn't. Sophie was in my head, and I could not get her out of my mind. If I tried to think about something else, I was thinking about something. If I tried not to think about anything, then I was thinking about her.

I don't know, at this point, I guess, people would say that I was in love with her. But it didn't feel like that. I didn't feel like that. I didn't look at her from a sexual point of view, and don't get me wrong, she was beautiful to me and to anyone who would look at her. I just had a sense of completeness. A peaceful, easy feeling, like the song would say. Sophie calmed me. I felt safe. Maybe in the same way that I thought she felt safe when we were at the table in the restaurant earlier.

It was already midnight by the time I got to my hotel. That would give me seven hours of sleep. Enough for me.

The following day, I arrived at Sophie's hotel. Nine o'clock. Sharp as a Swiss train. Well, actually, five minutes earlier, but Sophie showed up at the precise time. I got out of the car and opened the trunk so she could get her gear in. She put it in and gave me a hug.

"Ready to go?"

"Yes, I am ready."

"Ok, let's go. I drive, and you take care of navigation and music."

"Ok, fine. Where to?"

"To the mountains."

I handed her a piece of paper with the destination, and she plugged it into the GPS. We both were somehow desperate to get out of the city traffic and hit the open road. We arrived at our destination two hours later. Just in time to take the train to go up the mountain. It was a gorgeous, sunny day. No wind, no clouds, not too hot, a good day for some sightseeing on the top of the mountain.

We would walk and sit. Sit and talk. No stress. It was a day off. As the stories from her trips were coming to an end, the conversations turned a little bit more personal. Still with a great deal of caution. Both were eager to know more about each other but always kept a safe distance. Always with a lot of respect.

I noticed that Sophie was getting more and more pensive. There was more silence on her side. Not that it would bother me. I am comfortable in silence. I think we both were.

We spent the rest of the day at the mountain and got the last train back. We drove back to the city to a restaurant I had booked. Nothing fancy, but after a day at the mountain, I thought it would be nice to have a good dinner.

I picked a restaurant close to her hotel so we wouldn't have to drive long afterwards. It would be a short, nice walk to her hotel, so I thought it would be ok for her as well.

We had dinner and talked cheerfully, remembering our project and some of the funny moments in it. The main dishes came and went, and we were at the dessert already.

Sophie was enjoying her dessert when she paused and looked down, and after a few seconds, she asked.

"Can I ask you a question?"

"You know you can, why do you ask?"

"Not a normal question."

"It is ok, anything you want to ask, you can ask."

"Have you ever done something crazy?"

"What do you mean, crazy?"

"Crazy."

"Crazy like skydiving crazy, crazy like speeding on the highway crazy or crazier than that?"

"Crazier."

"Crazier? Ok, what level of craziness are we talking about here? Drugs? I've never done them. I'll never do them."

"No, no drugs."

"Then what?"

"A heist."

"Are you asking me to participate in a heist?"

"Somehow."

"A heist?!! You are not serious, are you?"

"Yes, I am."

I looked around to see who could be listening to this conversation. The restaurant was almost empty, and waiters were busy starting to get everything ready to close. As I saw no danger, I went back to the conversation.

"A heist! I mean, a heist? You know that is against the law in any country around the world, right? You have been in enough places to know that."

"Yes, I know, I know. But it is not what you think and stop saying that word!!"

"I don't get it. How come a heist is not a heist? Either it is, or it isn't."

She paused for a second, trying to find the right words to explain herself.

"Is it stealing if something is abandoned? Is it stealing if it is to get something that no one wants or that is not being used?"

"I don't know. If something has an owner, I guess it is still theft."

"What if it doesn't have an owner or the owner just doesn't want it?"

Darn! Sophie was always able to play these types of games with me. She would challenge normal thinking. Regular and well-known assumptions and ask the questions in a way that would keep me challenging my own straightforward answers.

"I…I don't know. I am not a lawyer, Sophie. I don't really know."

Sophie smiled as if she had accomplished something in the conversation. She knew I lived in ones and zeros. She knew I was not comfortable in grey areas. Things were or were not. However, I was already curious at this point, so I tried to indagate a little bit more.

"So, tell me. What were you planning to steal?"

"I cannot tell you yet."

"Where is it?"

"I don't know yet."

"You want me to help you steal something, but you don't know what it is yet, and you don't even know where it is. Am I correct?"

"I have some ideas."

"Well, is it big, small, heavy, light? What is it? A diamond, a picture, a car?"

"No, nothing of the sort."

"A horse?"

She smiled again, looked me in the eyes, and said, "Maybe one day."

A silence fell on the table for 30 seconds.

"Alvin, I'm tired. It has been a long, beautiful day, and thank you for the dinner. It was lovely. I have to fly out tomorrow. Would you take me to the airport?"

"Sure, sure. No problem. What time is your flight?"

"12.45 pm, but I'll need to be there at 10.15 am. It is a transatlantic flight."

"Ok, no problem. I'll pick you up at 8.30 am. It will be rush hour and we need to cross the whole city, and I don't want to be late. I mean, I don't want you to be late."

"I know you don't."

We walked the short distance to her hotel, and we hugged again. Always just a bit longer than normal. Always special to me somehow."

"Good night, Sophie."

"Good night, Alvin."

The last day in Barcelona was rainy. I met Sophie at the hotel at 8.30 am as promised. I put the few luggages she had in the trunk of the car, and we drove to the airport. She was noticeably quiet all the way. Just listening to the radio and looking through the window. I wondered what was going through her head but never dared to ask. I thought maybe it was the fact that we were going in different directions. Or maybe, she was thinking about her next trip. Or maybe she was thinking about the conversation from the previous night.

"You ok, Sophie?"

"Yes, I am ok."

She looked at me and gave me a light smile. I didn't ask more questions. I figured that there was enough trust between us for her to tell me what was going through her head if she wanted me to know. We were always so careful. I am not sure if it was just respect, or maybe fear of the wrong answer. Respect that we always had. The biggest. I think fear was something I saw growing. Don't get me wrong, it was not a fear of each other. I believe it was an internal fear. A fear of disappointing the other. I had mine, and she had hers.

We reached the airport. Sophie checked her backpack, and we found a place to sit at one of the bars in the departure hall.

"Madrid? Is it your next destination?"

"No, just a connecting flight."

"Where to?"

"The US. West Shore."

"It sounds like fun. I have never been that far."

"It will be the first time for me as well."

"Any plans over there?"

"You know me. Some culture and museums. Some photographs. I will also be meeting friends over there. They are flying in as well."

"That will be nice. At least you will have some good company."

"I can't complain about the one I have right now."

We stopped the conversation, and a long silence came down upon us again. We didn't say anything. Both of us reached the middle of the table, and we held each other's hands for the first time. No words were spoken. We just looked into each other's eyes and just held hands. Somehow, I think that was something we both wanted to do for a while. Part of our internal fears had been overcome.

Remember when I told you that I couldn't recall the feeling of the handshake the first time I met her? Obviously, this was not a handshake as it lasted for a long time. After all these years, it is still very clear in my mind, the feeling of her skin. I swear I could even tell her body temperature. Her skin was colder than mine. I moved my thumb in a horizontal direction, going back and forth over the same area. It was soft. Not slippery or oily. Neither dry. I gently pressed my thumb on her hand, feeling it. It seemed to me that her skin was swollen but elastic. Maybe because the temperature in the airport was quite high.

I guess people do these types of movements when holding hands. Most probably, everyone does it in an unconscious way. I didn't. I was aware of every movement I made. I was aware of every feeling I got back. Just as if it were a mathematical equation where every input generates an output, I was recording and memorising every single data point. That's how I remember that feeling so well.

We all get so many inputs every day through our senses that we just don't focus on them. I do. I focus. The touch, the smell, the moment, and I really value them in my head and most importantly, I exercise those memories not to forget them. I think that sets me apart from other people.

Sophie was taking a flight in less than an hour. I wasn't sure if I would see her again, and if I would, when would that be?"I have to go," Sophie said.

And we both slowly let our hands go. I walked her to the security area, and we hugged. This time for a long time. I rubbed my hand on her back, and I tapped her softly. I broke the hug because, otherwise, I would have never let her go.

"Please, be careful and take care. Let me know if you ever need anything."

"I will, Alvin."

She turned around, heading for the security check. She walked two steps and turned around to hug me again.

"Thank you, Alvin. I will let you know what's next."

With that, she crossed the security check this time and waved to me from the other side as she disappeared on the mechanical stairs.

I travel so much that I know the places in the airports or the surroundings to see the aeroplanes take off and land. I drove to the B-203 road. I parked the car, and I waited for Sophie's plane to take off. As her Airbus 321 roared out of the runway, it drowned out my sob and my tears.

I couldn't deny it anymore. At least not to myself. Sophie was a part of me, and it just broke me every time I saw her go away.

I spent the rest of the day watching the planes take off. Cursing every silence between the planes' departures. The silence allowed me to hear myself, and I didn't want to listen to my brain. Listen to my thoughts.

The end of the week came and now it was my time to fly out of Barcelona. I walked through the airport, trying to avoid all the places I had been to with Sophie the day before. I even walked to the far side of the airport to not go through the same security check she did. It was just ridiculous that I would do such a thing.

So ridiculous that I have never been back to Barcelona. I moved all the business discussions that I had there to somewhere else. It was also easy to find an explanation if someone asked. Explanations as excuses are always easy to come up with. The truth—the truth is always a trickier thing to come up with. The truth is always simple but difficult to explain or accept.

I was about to arrive home when I got a message from Sophie. She had arrived well in the US. Little did she know that I had monitored all her flights. There was nothing I could do or influence, but checking on her made me feel better. Although sometimes I felt bad about it. That was close to stalking.

I hit the bed early. I was exhausted. Not physically, but mentally. The number of feelings, sensations, conversations, and moments that I didn't want to lose in the basket of useless information with which I was bombarded every day was large. My mind would go for each of them carefully and place them in my brain. As if I were archiving and documenting all of them.

Memories are the only thing left when people are not around. I didn't want to have low-quality memories. I wanted to have 8K resolution memories. The best I could probably create. For that, you need to exercise. You need to bring your memories back. Revisit them. Make sure that they are being preserved in the most accurate way possible.

We need to be fair; we need to do this exercise with the good memories but also with the not-so-good ones. Bringing forward the memories of tears doesn't seem to be a great way to deal with things, but it was for me when I acknowledged where those tears were coming from.

Sophie being away made me sad, yes, but only because I got to meet her. I got to know her, and that sadness became joy.

Doing this exercise, I fell asleep with Sophie's words in my mind, "I will let you know what's next."

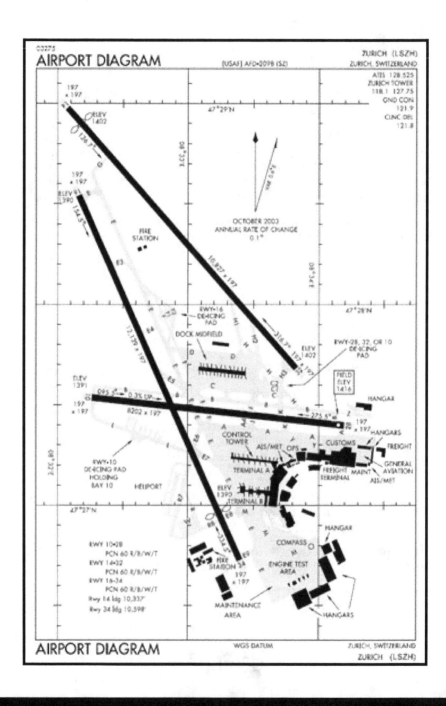

AIRPORT DIAGRAM

(USAF) AFD=2098 (SZ)

ZURICH (LSZH)
ZURICH, SWITZERLAND

ATIS 128.525
ZURICH TOWER
118.1 127.75
GND CON
121.9
CLNC DEL
121.8

OCTOBER 2003
ANNUAL RATE OF CHANGE
0.1°

AIRPORT DIAGRAM

WGS DATUM

ZURICH, SWITZERLAND
ZURICH (LSZH)

ZRH
ZURICH, SWITZERLAND

S ophie was gone. She was on the west coast of the United States. For a while, she wasn't keeping too much contact. My best guess was that she was having a great time with her friends on that side of the world. That's when I began to have an emotional roller coaster. I wanted her to keep in contact with me, but at the same time, I wanted to put some ground between us.

I always had the biggest respect for her. She was beautiful, smart, creative and funny, but I was always scared of her. She was one of the few people in this world who had been able to make me question myself. The only one who could challenge my logic and beat it. She had done it several times already on different topics. The most scary thing for me was the fact that she was able to do it with no effort. It would take her no time to find the right words to defy me. I never believed she did it with the intention of manipulating me or controlling me. She was just always trying for me to make me look at things in a unique way. It didn't mean that it had to be necessarily her way. Just a different way. But I missed her. I missed her a lot. However, I knew that she had to have her space, her friends, her trips, her time, her hobbies. I not only ever tried to control her, but I always encouraged her to find that space. Her own space away from me. I had learnt the hard way that not living your own life would never end well for anyone. You always need to have different lives. The ones you share and your own.

I know some people would think that that would be like cheating, having a parallel life that is not shared, but I now think that it is so necessary that no one can be in a relationship and survive without it. Everyone needs to have their own hobbies, friends, secrets, thoughts, dreams, hopes and even loved ones.

All these thoughts would hit me when I was not working.. Every night, every flight, every drive back and forth from airports or work, and any time I would be alone, it would open a reflection on all these topics. A reflection on Sophie. Sometimes, I would think about it very deeply other times, I would try to push it away from my mind. Most of the time without success.

The project I had been working on, since I finished the one with Sophie, was getting on a critical path. Pretty soon I would have to go to management and present it for approval. I had mixed feelings about it. On one hand, from a purely engineering perspective, it was very interesting, and I really would like it to be approved. If approved, the project would keep me busy for another 18 months. Therefore, my head would be occupied by it, and that way, I would avoid thinking about her so much.

On the other hand, I didn't have any desire to do the project without her. I mean, the person who took her role was okay. Nothing against her, but she wasn't Sophie, and my expectations on how to work around the project from a technical point of view and from a personal point of view were unrealistic. I knew it was not fair, and I always tried to keep that in mind. Thus, the job was accomplished but without complicity. I was doing my job without my partner, and although I put my best face on it, it wasn't the same. And I knew it. I couldn't lie to myself.

I was in a meeting at one of the suppliers in the south-west of Germany when my mobile rang.

"Alvin, speaking."

"Hi, there!"

"Sophie?"

"Yes, do you remember me?"

"Of course, I do. I was just not expecting your call right now."

"Oh, is it a bad time?"

"Ah? Eh, no, no, it is ok. Give me a sec. Don't go anywhere."

"Ok, I can wait."

I excused myself from the meeting I was having, and I stepped out of the building. I didn't think about it and went to the street wearing a shirt and nothing else. It was cold, very cold. At the end of the day, it was the end of December in Germany, and it doesn't get very warm there.

"Hi, Sophie, Are you there?"

"I am here, don't worry. How are you?"

"I am ok; I was just in a meeting with one of the suppliers for my project."

"Oh, should I call later?"

"Nah, it is ok. I left them in the meeting room, thinking about something that will keep them busy for a couple hours."

"Really? What did you tell them?"

"The standard. I told them that they have way too much faith in gravity, and I don't."

"Always keep the product under control, right?"

"Yeah, that's it. Always!"

Sophie always understood all my jokes. The way I would point to the suppliers what I would like to have but without telling them. That was the difference between Sophie and other people.

"I'm sure they are twisting themselves into pretzels, trying to figure that one out."

"I'm sure they are, but they are smart people, they will come up with something. How are you?"

"Great, I'm still in Los Angeles."

"How is it going over there?"

"It has been a great trip so far. Lots of fun."

"That is so good to hear. I'm glad you are having a good time with your friends.

"They left already. Look, I will be going back to Europe for the year end. Can we meet?"

"I will try. Where?"

"Munich."

"Munich?"

"Second week of January. Will you be able to do that?"

"I mean, I don't know. I don't even have my laptop with me to look at my diary."

"Please, Alvin. It is important. It is important to me."

"Ah…Yes, alright. I don't know how, but I'll be there."

"You promise?"

Although it had been a short chat, I was freezing. I couldn't get my brain to work properly, and I didn't even know how I would make that happen, but if it was important for Sophie for whatever reason she may have, I would make it happen somehow.

"I…I…Yes, I promise, I'll be there."

"Great, thank you. I'll book my flights then. I will give you a call before I fly out of the States."

"Yes, please, do that."

"Take care."

"Yeah, Sophie, take care of yourself too."

I went back to the meeting room, and I asked for a break and a coffee. I had a cup of coffee while the engineers were trying to explain to me how they would overcome their gravity faith. To tell the truth, I didn't pay too much attention. My body was still trying to recover its body temperature and my brain was still trying to reconcile the conversation with Sophie with the reality of dates, compromises and dairies.

Once my body temperature went back to normal, I resumed the meeting, trying to focus on the solution they were proposing. I had to take Sophie out of my brain. This was a three million euro machine. I could not afford to screw this one up. I still needed a job to pay the bills.

The meeting got over, and I had a 500 kilometre drive ahead of me, and it was dark already. It was okay as long as the cold wouldn't turn into snow. Everyone says how mobile phones, GPS or calls can get you distracted when driving. No one talks about your own thoughts. I drove and got to my destination past midnight. I truly can't recall how I got there. I can't recall the highways, the towns, the exit ramps, the traffic, the radio in the background. I can't. I can only say that all the way I was thinking about Sophie. Why did she call? What was the hurry? What was so important for her? Why Munich? In summary, why me? She knew tons of people. Probably most of them were much more interesting than me. She had close friends. Sophie and I barely know each other from working together, the days we spent in Barcelona and holding hands in an airport once. There were so many questions I had that I was not able to answer. I could not even define the line between us. In any case, if there were a line, it would be very fine.

Now, all that was left for me was to wait for Sophie to call before leaving the States. If there were something you could take for granted with Sophie, it was that if she said she would do something, that something would happen. A 100 per cent guaranteed. It wouldn't matter if it was work or personal. She would have to be dying for her not to fulfil her word, and I love that about her. That, and the fact that she was always on time.

And sure enough, a couple days later, I got her call.

"Hi, Alvin."

"Hi, Sophie."

"Everything ok for you these days?"

"Yes, all good, you know…work."

"I have my tickets already."

"Cool, which flights?"

"I knew you would ask, so here I have my cheat sheet. Are you ready to copy?"

"Go for it!"

"On 16 December, SFO to ATL on DL 570 at 06:00 PST, and then ATL to MUC on DL 130 at 17:55 EST, arriving at MUC at 09:00 CET the following day."

"Got it!"

Sophie knew that I would just be the only person she knew who could get the message delivered and understand all the acronyms in it."

"You know I will track the flights, right?"

"Yes! I know you always do."

"I don't mean stalking here, just wanted to make sure that…"

"I know, Alvin. I always appreciate it. I really do. Thanks. Are you still on your promise to go to Munich in the second week of January?"

"Yes, I am. I have arranged a meeting to present my project on 11 January in Zurich at the head office, so I can be in Munich the following morning and stay there the rest of the week. Would that work for you?"

"That is just perfect, Alvin. Thanks for making those dates. It is really important for me."

"I know you mentioned that. In fact, I wanted to ask you about that. The dates, the place, why are they so important? I mean, you know, you asked me to be there, and I will. Even if you don't want to explain it, I will be there anyway. You know it, don't you?"

"I do. Look, I can't talk about it right now. There are too many people around, and I don't feel comfortable talking about it with people around me. Let me get back to Munich and settle there for a couple of days, then I will call you and explain."

It was clear to me that I was not going to get my answer at that moment. Pressing the issue would not help, so I let it go with a sigh. That's all I could do.

I did track her flight and made sure that she would get through the whole journey safe and well. A short message from Sophie confirmed it.

I let her go for a couple of weeks. Besides, Christmas was upon us, and I am not the best person to be around during those dates. Not that I had any trauma at Christmas. It was more about the number of people that always gathered everywhere. The established things that everybody is supposed to take part in and actually enjoy them. I didn't. Good to see the family, but I also see them during the year and no big deal is made of that. Everything seems to be too forced.

Somehow, I had to make it through another Christmas season without losing my sanity and without getting into conversations or conflicts I would regret later. So being quiet, or I would say extra quiet, most probably would take me over the season and the New Year's celebration. The only prospect of the new year was for Sophie to call and start clearing up the mystery she had around the second week of January and Munich. Well, that and my project presentation, but that was under control because it was under my control. Not the outcome, but the work towards that presentation.

The new year came, and two days into it, I got the promised call from Sophie.

"Hey, happy New Year!"

"Hi, happy New Year to you too. All good for you these days? Settling in?"

"Yes. All good here. Christmas and New Year are always times to reflect and plan. I don't take those things lightly as you well know. How were your holidays?"

"You know, not special for me. Just another two weeks to live."

"Oh, come on, I'm sure it was not all that bad."

"I guess I can say it was ok. I didn't get myself into trouble, which is already an accomplishment. Look, I wanted to ask you about the upcoming weeks."

"Yes, and you deserve to know. Remember our conversation in Barcelona?"

"Which one of them? We spent almost three days together having conversations."

"And walks and silences."

"Yes, and silences."

"The conversation we had at the restaurant the night before I left. The one about doing crazy things."

"Oh! that one. The one about a heist you didn't know what and didn't know where or when."

"But now I have more clarity on those three questions."

"Do you?"

"I would like you to help me. To join me in this enterprise."

"Enterprise? Sophie! This is not like we are trying to set up a start-up business. We are talking about stealing."

"Again, I am not talking about stealing as such. I am talking about having ownership of something that has been abandoned. Unwanted."

"But what is it?"

"A small piece of jewellery. Easy to take, carry and hide. It will be in Munich in the second week of January. It is just the perfect timing."

"So, what do you need me for?"

"I need you to cover me and drive me out. It will be worth it."

"I…I need to think about all this, Sophie. This is just so crazy for me. I can't even rationalise this in my head. I need some time to get my brain around this."

"It is not so difficult, Alvin. We go, we take it, we walk out and we disappear."

"That simple?"

"Yes, that simple. I just need to know if you are in or not. Think about it and come back to me with your decision. If you are, I'll share more details. Otherwise, I can't. It wouldn't be safe for me."

"Ok, yeah, I mean, I will come back to you with something."

"Just remember, it will have to be in the second week of January, or the deal is off. And I need to have an answer by January 12th, noon. I can't stress this point enough."

"Clear."

"Ok, bye, Alvin."

I hung up and was left with a conundrum I was not even sure I would be able to solve. There were 12 days until I would arrive in Munich. So that was my time limit. I got my car and went for a drive to the mountains. Although I knew a drive was not going to solve this one. This one was going to take something else to figure out.

To tell the truth, I decided not to think about it too much and focus on work. I have never been particularly good at managing more than one complex project at a time. Sophie meant a lot to me, so I just couldn't put her proposal on the back burner till the last minute, so questions and answers popped in and out of my brain through the following days.

I decided to fly to Zurich on Sunday night. That way, I would be busy and not think, and at the same time, I would have a proper rest for my presentation on Monday morning.

I arrived on the 6 pm flight. Zurich on a Sunday night doesn't have too many things open. I took the tram and rode the short two-stop distance to my destination. I booked a hotel next to the head office, which was basically at the airport itself. So close that planes flew low over the hotel, which always made for an amazing view.

I checked in and went downstairs to have something for dinner. Only the Asian restaurant was open in the hotel. Thus, the choice was easy: Asian or the old club sandwich available everywhere in Europe. I went for Asian, although I was not really a fan of it, and I always struggled a bit with the chopsticks.

I have travelled for work a lot throughout my career. A lot of countries and cities in Europe, and some overseas. I think what I always hated the most was having dinner alone. I was always in a hurry to finish my dinner and get out of the restaurant. I didn't like people staring at me at a one-person table. I went through the process of having dinner as soon as I could, and then I went back to my room.

I reviewed the presentation for the following day. I had gone through it a hundred times already, and I knew it by heart. However, I am an engineer. I can see the problem, and I can provide the solution. I was never good at selling the solution. For me, there was nothing to sell. In my head, I didn't have to convince anyone that that solution was the best. It was the best and only one. In particular, for this project, you just couldn't prevent the laws of physics from getting their way. Still, I was realistic about the fact that there would be directors and marketing people in the meeting who basically live in a different space and time. The discussions with them were not technical discussions but rather financial or perception discussions. Those were so different from engineering that I had learned to bite my tongue and not get into a war where I had no arguments to win. Just in case and to remind myself constantly of that fact, I kept on my mobile an on-screen message to myself, "Think twice and be quiet." Ah! That sentence has kept me away from so many unnecessary discussions and arguments that I would never be able to thank myself enough for it.

I went to bed early, and I fell asleep almost right away. I never thought about Sophie, or about her proposal, or about what my outcome of that would be. I had always been exceptionally good at putting things in the corner of my head and ignoring them, regardless of how hard or painful those things were. I would put them there and ignore them. I believe what is in your head will only hurt you if you let them do it. For that night, I put Sophie in a corner of my brain, but that was a temporary parking spot and I knew she wouldn't be there for long. I didn't like her to be in a corner. There were way too many things about Sophie that I wanted to know, and although her proposal puzzled me in an imaginable manner, she was too interesting and vexed me way too much for me to ignore her. However, for that night, I had to. I had no choice. I couldn't screw up a year-and-a-half of work. As I said, I still needed to pay my bills.

I woke up the next morning without thinking that that week would change my life from a professional and personal point of view. I took a shower and went downstairs for breakfast. I had a good one. I couldn't go into this day with a half-empty stomach. I picked up my gear and crossed the road to the head office. I went around saying hi to the known people and looked for the meeting room to present my project.

The meeting started, and it went as planned. No one argued about the solution and soon enough the discussions turned into financial and perception ones as I had predicted. I kept myself quiet and away from discussions that were not mine unless asked for. I think I did a good job until someone asked for a break, and I was called to the office of one of the managers of the region.

"Alvin, there is no way we are going to pay three million for that line."

"Yes, you will, if you want to have the problem solved for good."

"It is too expensive. The company will not do it. You need to do it cheaper."

"It can't be done if you want a guarantee to solve the problem 100 per cent."

"I will ask someone else to look at it."

"I really don't know what I am getting paid for. The company pays me to solve the problem. I do solve the problem, I give the best possible cost and you don't want to accept it and want to give the project to someone else. Do it. Whoever it is, if they know what they are doing, they will come back with the same solution."

We went back to the meeting room and finalised the meeting. I didn't say a word until the meeting was over, then I said my farewells to people. I still cannot explain how I didn't get fired that day. Believe it or not, I didn't. They never went ahead with the project, and they still have the same problem. But the fact that the company decided not to go for the project got me thinking about what would be next for me. I was not willing to go on small and meaningless projects. I really needed to think about what to do with my career.

However, now that the work theme was over, I needed to focus my mind on Sophie. I had less than 24 hours to come back to her with an answer to her proposal.

I went for a walk. It was cold and dark. I walked with no real destination. I tried not to think about anything. Not work, not Sophie. I was just trying to empty my head of any thoughts. I was getting close to that state of emptiness when a loud roar got me out of my state. I looked up and saw only a white light moving across the sky. It was foggy, and I couldn't see anything, but being as close to the airport as I was, that could only be a plane taking off. A large one. Anyone, I kept walking, trying to recover my state, but it was not useful. The roar of the plane had just taken me back to reality, where I had to make a decision about Sophie and her plan. I could walk more, but I thought I had postponed the matter long enough and a decision had to be made.

I went back to the hotel and had a light dinner. I was sitting alone in the restaurant and watching the other tables. People sitting alone were of no interest to me. I focused more on the tables where men and women shared the space. Some of the tables had a loud conversation going on. On others, the conversation was at a quieter level. In others, there were no conversations. Looking at the expressions of the people during the conversations, you could almost tell if they were talking about work or private stories. Then, within the private conversations, impressions of joy, sadness, and indifference could be told apart. The details are there. It is just a matter of looking for them. I had never been good at the detail level. At least, not at my job anyway. However, when it came to people, all these details started to pop up in front of me as something easy to read.

The restaurant became empty slowly, and the waiter's look told me that I should leave already and let them close for the day. So, I sighed, stood up and walked to my room. I prepared the luggage for the early flight to Munich the next morning and began to look out the window.

Darn! What was I going to do? What was I going to do with Sophie, with her proposal, with her, with me?

I began running scenarios in my head like a computer would. What would be the outcome if I went for her plan? What would be the consequences? I help her and then what? Would I move on with her? Would she accept or reject me? What if she would? What if she wouldn't? Where do I go from there? And then what? Do we keep making heists? Was this a one-off? Why only one? Would it be more? What would happen to me, to my career, to my job, to my world? Would I lose Sophie if I said no? What if…?

God, the number of scenarios and possibilities were just too large for my brain to hold all their possible answers. So, I sat down and pulled a piece of paper and a pen from the room desk. I began creating flowcharts. Trying to rationalise all the thoughts I had. I filled probably 20 pages. Pages that I had to review to make sure I was not missing anything in the analysis.

I was getting really frustrated. I couldn't figure out the right answer if there was one to be found. I took a break and a shower, hoping that I would get a hint under the water that would solve this puzzle. I stepped out of the shower with no hint.

I went to the desk, and I crushed all the papers before throwing them in the waste. I lay on the floor and began to do my relaxation exercises. I had learned them back in the university days. Actually, it was a mandatory course for all students attending the university back in the States. Maybe, one of the most, if not the most, useful courses I ever took. The only one I had used throughout my career.

After 30 minutes, I checked my smartwatch and saw my heartbeat coming down to 60 heartbeats per minute. A good indication that the exercise has worked. I slowly got up and restarted my analysis. I went through everything all over again. Same ideas, some new. I made new charts. I considered new possibilities, new variables, new iterations. I sorted them in terms of probabilities, and then, I once again crushed all the papers and put them in the bin.

I rested my head against the window glass and looked outside. It was dark and rainy. I looked at the clock. It was 1.37 am. At that precise time, at 1.37 am in that hotel in Zurich, for the first time in my life, I got a sense of being alone in this world. Helpless, hopeless, lost, with no direction, with no plan. I have always been a quiet person. Not too many friends in my life. Not too many interactions with other people. I somehow liked to be on my own. I liked it that way, but it was my choice. Now it was different. It was as if I had the responsibility of the entire world on my shoulders. The feeling that the decision I had to make about Sophie would determine the fate of everyone I knew and even people I didn't even know.

I couldn't think clearly anymore. I was stuck. I decided that my brain had had enough, and I went into bed. The flight to Munich was at 8 am so that would give me only four hours of sleep.

I don't think I fell asleep. I had the feeling that I just got unconscious and passed out the moment I closed my eyes. It had been six hours of an exhausting battle in my head.

That night in Zurich is marked in my head as one of the most memorable nights of my life. A night I remember today with a lot of sadness as it showed my fragility, my vulnerability. A feeling of no longer being in control of things. Never had it before, never had it again, or at least not like that. I was a strong person until that night. After that, I changed. I never felt like myself anymore.

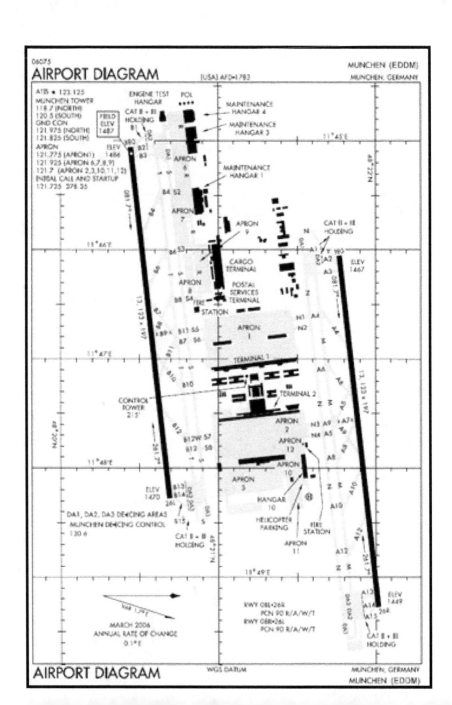

4

MUC
MUNICH, GERMANY

The alarm went off. I woke up very tired. Still in bed, I review the schedule in my head.

6.30 am Check out of the hotel

7.00 am Arrive at the airport

7.30 am Board

8.00 am Take off

8.55 am Land

9.15 am Drive to city centre

10.00 am Arrive at the city centre. Allow 30 minutes for rush hour.

10.30 I am meeting Sophie and…and then, what?

There was no way to know. I had not made a decision or a plan yet. I couldn't restart the analysis process again, or I would never make it to the airport. I got out of bed, had a shower, and stuck to the agenda.

I went through airport security and had a coffee. Under other circumstances, I would have driven. It is only 360 km, but traffic is heavy getting out of Zurich, and then you need to go briefly through Austria before getting into Germany, just to find more heavy traffic once you pass Memmingen. Too risky. Sophie had set a deadline at noon, and I had to be there with or without an outcome. I boarded the plane and sat down by the window. I fell asleep. The next thing I remember was the noise of the tyres touching down in Munich. That was an additional 55 minutes of more than needed sleep.

I got my luggage and went to pick up my rental car. I used to travel so much that I had an upgraded car. It was an impressive Jaguar F-Type convertible. I would have taken the car without thinking, but for some reason, Sophie's proposal came to my mind. Maybe this sort of car is not the best choice if you are going to make a heist and you want to go through the city unadvertised. I went back to the rental office and asked for the car to be changed. I had to come up with some sort of credible excuse to turn down such a car. In the end, I asked for a Volkswagen Golf TDI, arguing that I needed an economical car with luggage space and a good range, as I was going to drive many kilometres. There were thousands of cars like that in Munich, so it would be just another one.

I checked the traffic in the GPS, and I messaged Sophie, "On my way. I will arrive at 10.15 am, Pariser Pl."

The morning was grey and cold. The standard in Munich during the wintertime. I parked the car near the train station, and I walked to the meeting point. I saw Sophie from a distance. She was wearing a blue jacket and her blonde hair stood out against the general grey.

"Hi."

"Hi."

She gave me a hug. It was a short, cold hug. Quite different from the ones in Barcelona. I broke the hug as soon as she did. I looked at her, and she had a serious face. Not a trace of a smile, and she looked tired. I felt something was off, but I didn't want to start a conversation in the middle of the street. So, I kept it brief and just asked her, "Should we go?"

Sophie just nodded and we began walking to a small café in street nearby. She had booked a table. We sat down, and I began looking at the menu. She didn't. I thought maybe she wasn't hungry. The waiter came and took the order. I got some scrambled eggs, bacon, orange juice and black coffee. She ordered some toast, tea and a mixed fruit juice. Clearly, she had been in the place before, and she knew the menu by heart.

There was no feeling whatsoever. Not a trace of the colleague I worked with in the past or the person I met later in Barcelona. She was just quiet, as if she were not there. I couldn't understand very well at that moment what was going on. I couldn't understand if it was fear or if she was going through something. I could only see that she was tense, nervous. Yes, that could be the way to describe her. The feeling when you are nervous, but you are doing your best to hold yourself together. Trying to control your movements, your expressions, your words.

I broke the silence as the situation was becoming too uncomfortable.

"So, how have you been?"

"I have been doing ok. Keeping myself busy. And you?"

"You know, work, meeting, travelling…"

"How was yesterday's meeting?"

"That didn't land well at all, but, you know, not my money, not my problem."

"Yeah, right. So, what is your problem?"

"What do you mean?"

"I mean…never mind."

The waiter interrupted as she came with the food and placed it on the table. We were sitting at 90 degrees. She was sitting on a bench. I was to her left on a chair."

We started eating in silence at the beginning. After a while, she looked at me with a sad face and asked,

"Why are you here?"

"You asked me to come, right?"

"Yes, I did. You know why I asked you to come, right?"

"Yes, I know."

I looked down. I knew. I knew that I had landed, driven from the airport, met her and walked into the cafe without a plan. Without a decision. Even more, at this point, there was nothing in my head. I was completely blank. As if every thought that came through my mind was unbiased. I was unable to coordinate or articulate any phrase. I couldn't say yes to her proposal, and I couldn't say no. I looked straight into her blue eyes. I could read her disappointment and her sadness. I will never be able to explain what happened next.

I held her left hand with my right hand. I stood up. I bent until I met her face, and I kissed her lips softly, and then I kissed her in the same manner for a second time. I held my face in front of her until she opened her eyes so she would meet mine. I didn't say anything, and I sat back in my chair while still holding her hand.

Her expression changed from sadness to an expression of incredibility and confusion. No smile was to be found on her face. I guess in her mind, she had pictured a conversation. I don't believe she was expecting my reaction. Our eyes kept in contact for some time until she looked down and resumed eating her brunch. I let her hand go, and I resumed mine.

Maybe my best plan to resolve the proposal that Sophie had given me was not to have a plan and just let go. I could not tell until the moment I held her hand and kissed her, which direction the no-plan would go. There was no premeditation in any of my actions. It was pure improvisation and just does.

That wasn't me, but I felt so good. So unbelievably good. I refused to think about what those actions could bring upon me. To this date, I have not regretted that kiss. Not a single day of my life after have I regretted it, and I will never do.

I looked at the clock on the wall. 10.53 am. I tried to locate myself in space. Time and space are coordinates. I would remember them. Life is about moments, instants, and precise infinitesimal points of data. This instant will be one to remember.

We finished our brunch without talking. Just crossing looks once in a while. I think Sophie was still processing the last 15 minutes, but I could be wrong and maybe her headspace was elsewhere.

I took the bill and we put on our coats before getting out of the I.

"Should we go for a walk?"

"I think it is too cold for a walk."

"Is there any place we can go inside?"

She thought for a second and checked her phone.

"Yes, there is a museum nearby."

"That will do it."

Sophie searched for my hand and held it once she found it. We started to walk slowly down the street, and I let her guide me to the museum. Her expression was more relaxed. Now it was as if she were concentrating on something else. Whatever it was, it was not stressing her.

We went inside the museum and began our way through the exhibition. Sophie was still holding my hand as we walked. The museum was almost empty, as Tuesday morning didn't seem to be a popular time. We arrived at a big room with a seating space in the middle. We sat, and for the first time in the day, Sophie smiled a little and said,

"So, that kiss means that you are in?"

"I'm in."

"You just could have said yes."

"I couldn't find the courage for that."

"Oh, Alvin, you are hilarious. You couldn't find the courage to say yes, but you managed to find the courage to kiss me twice. Any normal person would have said yes or no."

"You know I am far from being normal."

"Yes, you are far from a normal guy. You are unusual, I guess."

"I guess I am. So, now that I am in, are you going to share the details with me? I would like to know what I have signed myself for."

"Fair enough. It is a small piece of jewellery. In a small box. Easy to take, easy to carry around, easy to hide. It is in an apartment. I will take it. You will wait and drive me out. You have a car, don't you?"

"Yes, I have. How will you get into the apartment? Is there anyone there?"

"You can leave that with me but no one will be there."

"But there will be no violence. If there is violence, the deal is off, and I'm out."

"There will be no violence. I can assure you of that. If there were, I wouldn't do it. I'm not a violent person. As I said, it has no owner and no one wants it."

"I'm still struggling with the 'no owner, no one wants it' part."

"Trust me, it is like that."

"But why? Is it valuable? Do you do it for the money?"

"Yes, it is valuable, but I'm not doing it for the money."

"Then why?"

"For the same reason, you kissed me."

"I don't understand."

"You don't need to, but enough of this, we have work to do."

"Ok, what is the plan?"

"It will happen tomorrow morning. Now, we'll take the car. We will drive there, and we will plan the escape route."

"Tomorrow!?"

"Yes, it has to be tomorrow."

Let's go, then. I don't want to drive at night."

We left the museum and walked to the train station. We reached the parking lot and approached the rental car. The lights blinked as I pressed the bottom of the remote. Sophie looked at me and said,

"A Golf!? Really? You are kidding me, right? We are going for a heist, and you rented a Golf as an escape car? It is not even a GTI model. It is just a regular diesel one."

"Well, I had the opportunity to get a two-door SuperSport Jaguar convertible."

"Why didn't you?"

"I thought it would draw too much attention. Besides, this is not a movie. I am not going to make an escape at 160 km/h through the city with a bunch of BMW police cars chasing me. I am not Jason Statham, and this is not The Transporter. Get real. A dull car like this would let us go through the city unnoticed."

"I guess you are right. Yeah, I think this is a better choice, but don't deny that the Jaguar would have been a much more glamorous and far cooler choice."

"I don't deny it, but we need to be practical."

"Wait! Wait a minute! Did you change the car because you had already made your decision at the airport to say yes and join me?"

"No. As I said, I hadn't made the decision, but I thought that I should cover all possibilities, just in case. I went to the cafe with no-plan whatsoever. It turned out like this."

"Sometimes, it is impossible to follow your reasoning."

"Don't feel bad, sometimes I can't either."

We jumped into the car and drove to the street.

"Where are we? Is it here?"

"Yes, park the car and we will walk the rest of the way. We are near Olympia Park."

"Olympia Park? This is on the outskirts of the city, isn't it?"

"Yes. We will escape into the city rather than out of it. Let's review the plan. We will arrive here at 11 am. I will get out of the car, get into the apartment, get the box. In the meantime, you will wait in the car in this area. I will be back at 11.10."

"Ten minutes? That's it?"

"How long do you think it would take to get into the apartment and take a small case?"

"I...I don't know. What happens if someone comes to where I will be waiting?"

"You will be alright. You can park there for 15 minutes. I will be back long before anyone can bother you."

"What if you are late?"

"I won't. I will be back in ten minutes."

"And then?"

"Then we will drive into the city. We will park the car at the Museum Brandhorst. There is a nature photography exhibition that I wanted to see. Also, no one will look for us there…or anywhere. No one will know."

"No one will?"

"Alvin, remember when we worked on the project, and I ran into a problem, and you asked me to trust you?"

"I remember."

"I trusted you because I knew you could be trusted. I trusted you because if someone could find a solution, you would be the one doing it. Even if I couldn't understand it. Now it is your turn to trust me. Will you?"

"Yes, I'll trust you."

"Good. Let's drive to the museum, so you are familiar with the route."

We made it to the museum in no time.

"Remember, Dachauer Str and Gabelsbergerstraße and then left onto Türkenstraße. Straight, straight, left. Easy!"

"It is easier when you say it like that instead of the street's names!"

"Hahaha. Sure, ok, let's make it all over again."

We made the ride three times until I was able to do it without hesitation. I had memorised the streets and the turns. I was confident that I could do it without issues.

"Well, I think I have mastered this, don't you think?"

"Yes, you have, Alvin. Now I have an escape plan all set."

"I need to go and check into my hotel and have some rest. It has been a long two days, and I need to be fresh for tomorrow."

Sophie held my hand as I was going to set the first gear and paused for a moment.

"Wait. No. Stay with me. Please."

"I have the hotel booked already."

"I know, but stay with me. You can stay in my apartment. Besides, a hotel leaves a trace with the registration and all that. If you don't show up, no one will be able to tell if you were in Munich or not."

"Fine. Where to?"

She guided me through the city. It didn't take long to arrive, but I could not tell where I was. I parked the car and took my luggage to her apartment. It was a small apartment with only one room and a small living room connected to the kitchen. I looked around and couldn't find a space to place my backpack and my suitcase, without having the feeling of leaving them right in the middle of the whole apartment.

"Where do I put this?"

"Ah, just there against the window. Are you hungry? I can prepare something for dinner quickly."

"I am hungry, but I would like to have a shower first if that is ok with you."

"Sure, right there in the bedroom."

I went into the bedroom. Everything was so tidy and clean. I was somehow scared to touch or do anything to disturb the hyper-organised space. I got into the bathroom, undressed, and stepped into the shower. I stayed there under the hot water for a while, trying to relax my muscles and give my brain a break.

"Hey! Are you drowning in there? Dinner is ready."

"Yes, I mean, no. I mean, I am ok. I'll be out in a second."

I got out of the shower and put on some comfortable clothes. Sophie had the table ready.

"Sit down. I got ready for a salad with nuts, some cheese, bread, and ham. I hope you like it, and it is enough. I was not expecting visitors tonight."

"Of course you weren't. Don't worry. I'm flexible. I eat just about anything. It is good enough for me."

We ate a light dinner, mostly talking about Barcelona, my work, my travels. Sometimes, Sophie would laugh about a comment or a past memory, and she would hold my hand. I helped her with the dishes, and we moved into the living room. We sat on the sofa and kept chatting for a while until we both felt it was somehow getting late.

"I think we need to call it off tonight, don't you think so?"

"Yes, I think so. I can sleep here on the sofa."

"Don't be silly, Alvin."

She grabbed my hand and took me to the bedroom. We took turns in the bathroom and got into the bed.

"Thanks for coming, Alvin. You know that kiss at the cafe was really something. I have secretly looked for it, but you are not easy to read."

"I know I am not. I'm sorry."

"Don't. That's what makes you special."

She got close to me and kissed me. Then, we had sex. Correction, we just shared time together. There was sex, sure, but the caring I got from Sophie, it was something special. I don't think I have ever been with another woman before or after that gave me that feeling of caring. I think she was enjoying the feeling of giving and sharing as much as I was receiving it.

We fell asleep almost immediately. I slept through the night. I'm so used to travelling that I don't miss my bed anymore. Any decent place will do it and Sophie's fulfilled the criteria by a long shot. Not taking into account, her company.

"Wake up, sleepy head! We have a heist to execute!"

I opened my eyes and allowed five seconds to locate myself. Munich, Sophie, her apartment, the heist. She came and sat down on the bed.

"Good morning! How do you feel? Did you get some rest?"

"I certainly did."

"Are you ready?"

"I will after I have a coffee and something to eat."

"I got that. Breakfast is on the table."

"Perfect."

I got out of bed and we both had breakfast. A coffee, some toast, some fruit. That would make it to lunchtime, whenever that turned out to be. I took a shower and put my clothes on.

"Sophie! What do you think a heist calls for? The blue Oxford shirt or a more informal T-shirt and hoodie?"

"You are such a fool! Get the blue shirt. I like that one on you."

"Done."

We left her apartment, got in the car, and drove to Olympia Park.

"Turn right here."

"Here? We are not there yet. Are we changing the plan?"

"No, we are actually sticking to the plant. We are early. We need to make some time, and it is better to drive around the block here than in the block where the apartment is."

"Good thinking."

We drove around the same block for about ten minutes. Not speaking too much. I was watching the traffic and Sophie was…I am not sure what Sophie was thinking, but it was probably about getting everything perfect and according to her plan.

"It is time, let's go." I parked the car exactly at 11.00 am and in the exact spot Sophie had asked me to during the practice run the day before.

"Wish me luck!"

"Good luck!"

Sophie kissed me, and she stepped out of the car. She entered the building, and I began counting the seconds on my watch. Time goes by very slowly when you are looking at it. At 11.10 am, Sophie came out of the building as she had promised and jumped into the car.

"Go, go, go!"

"Easy, Sophie! Let's stick to the plan. Let's drive carefully and no one will notice us."

I started the car and drove, repeating the trip from the day before. Straight, straight, left. I merged into the traffic at Dachauer Str and drove until I got to the roundabout, and then straight again into Gabelsbergerstraße until I reached Türkenstraße, where I turned left as per the plan. I parked the car in a garage and turned to Sophie, as she had been quiet all along.

"Are you ok?"

"Uh?"

"Ok? Are you ok, Sophie?"

"Yes. Yes. Yes, I'm ok. Let me catch my breath, or my heartbeat, or both."

"Sure, no problem. We are safe here. Take your time."

"Ok, good, I am good. Let's walk into the museum."

"Yes, let's go."

We went into the museum and began our walk through the different galleries. We went through the first few quickly. Too fast. The plan was to stay there most of the morning.

"Let's take it easy, Sophie. Why don't we sit here for a while?"

"Yes, yes. Let's sit down."

Sophie took a long breath and looked at me with a mischievous smile.

"I told you it was going to be easy."

"Yes, you did, everything went according to your plan."

"How do you feel?"

"I feel…good? It is a weird sensation that I cannot describe."

She got close to me and kissed me.

"Thank you. You are the best. I would not have been able to do it without you. I would have only done it with you."

"So, can I see it?"

"Eh? No. I think it is better if you don't see it so you can keep your innocence."

"I'm not sure what that is supposed to mean."

"I was the one who took it. You can always claim that you didn't know and that you were just asked to drive."

"Hmmm…I don't know if that would be held in court, but anyway, it is ok."

"Yes, don't argue over this. It is done, we are safe, and we are together."

Sophie seemed to be much more relaxed as time went by. Me, on the other hand, I was still in a numbed state as I had not yet processed what had happened just a couple hours ago. To be honest, I thought it would be better not to even think about it and ignore the whole thing. I took Sophie to a place, and I picked her up 10 minutes later. That was all.

We went through a gallery where there were photographs of seals and we stood still in front of them. There was a big picture that stood out among the rest. I looked closer at the details.

"Did you see the photographer in the picture, Sophie?"

"No, what do you mean?"

"The photographer is in the iris of the seal. Do you see it?"

Sophie got closer and closer until she saw it. She looked at me puzzled.

"How were you able to spot that? How did you get that level of detail? I bet no one has seen that before. I thought you said that you were a person who only saw the forest, not the details. Not even at work during the project, you cared once about them."

"Yes, I know. I don't know. I just sometimes do."

"Sometimes."

"Yes. Sometimes. I think it is time for us to go. We haven't heard anything in the news. Let's go back to your apartment."

Sophie nodded her head, and we left the museum. We drove a couple of times around the block of her apartment. We wanted to check that no police or suspicious cars were parked. All seemed clear, but still, we parked the car further away and walked the rest.

"I'm going to have a shower, Alvin."

"Sure. Then we can go for dinner somewhere. What do you feel like having? Asian? Indian? Bavarian?"

"Asian sounds good to me."

"Deal. Let me find a nice place to go. We both deserve a nice dinner."

Sophie finished her shower and dressed up. It was a simple dress, but it really looked great on her. She always wore simple clothes, but they were always very well combined. Elegant but comfortable.

We walked to the restaurant as it was not very far away, and I thought burning a little bit of stress by walking would relax the both of us. Once at the restaurant, we ordered our food, and she held my hand.

"Do you remember when we met?"

"Of course, I do."

"At that time, you did not impress me at all. You really looked at me as a below-average man. I didn't think too highly of you."

"Really? So much for a first impression! Hahaha!"

"Really. You didn't seem to be very smart or funny or caring. For sure, not a person who would be bright at anything. But then, when you want to, with whom you want to, you unilaterally decide to shine, and you become this highly competent person, capable of holy cow ideas, able to solve almost any problem that you are given. You suddenly are the funniest person to be around, with a great, sharp sense of humour, and you transform yourself into the most loving, caring, and sweetest person I have ever met. And then, you are gone. As if you don't want people to know that part of you. As if you don't want people to know that you are smart, funny, caring. You just keep it to yourself instead, and even when you decide to share that part of you, it is like a shooting star. Ten seconds over the dark night sky and then gone."

I looked down at the table. I know Sophie was smart. I had worked with her; I had been with her long enough to know that. She had just stripped me bare in less than 30 seconds. I hated it. I hated that she was able to read me like that, but at the same time, I loved the fact that she had put the brain time to analyse me.

"I guess everyone has more than one side."

"Yes, we all do. I do as well, as you know."

"I know."

"But it is fun. It is an exploration game."

"What happens when the exploration is over? Is the game over?"

"I don't know. I have never played the game to the end. In any case, as for you, first, I don't think it will ever be possible for me to explore all of you. I don't think you would ever reveal all of you, and even if you do, you will keep reinventing yourself."

"Would that be a problem?"

"I don't know. On one hand, I believe that everyone needs to have their own secrets in their own life, even if they are in a relationship. If they give up a 100 per cent, I think they will stop developing themselves, and they will reach the end of their journey, and that relationship will fail. On the other hand, it will always be challenging to understand how much you know about the other person."

"I guess it will be a matter of wait and see as one goes."

The food arrived, and we switched the conversation to more irrelevant topics, as I cannot recall them. We went back to her apartment after we were done with dinner, and we got in bed.

"You know I need to get back tomorrow, right?"

"Shhhh...I don't want to hear about it."

With that, she softly kissed me, and once again we made love. Although it was just the second time, we were into it, it felt to me like the first one. The caring, the tenderness, the way she touched me. It was the same intensity, the same feeling of sharing and giving. I really felt loved. I really did. She filled my need of affection. I could only hope that she would feel the same way because I really cared about her. I always really tried to show it to her, but as Sophie said, I was not very good at showing things sometimes, though that didn't mean they were not there.

The thought of not giving her enough or of not being able to show my care and love for her would always haunt me. I really do love her.

The next morning, I woke up earlier. Sophie was still sleeping. I had a morning shower and prepared my luggage. I sat down on the bed and looked at Sophie in her sleep. Breathing slowly. Just looking at her sleeping like that really slowed my heart. I ran my fingers through her thin, blond hair. I whispered.

"Hey. Sophie."

"Hi."

"We need to get going."

"I know. Give me two minutes, I'll get ready."

"Sure. Don't stress, there is enough time."

We took the car and returned to the rental car stop. On our way to the terminal, we passed next to the Jaguar.

"This was it."

"Oh, Alvin, next time we will get this one! If I have to go to jail one day, at least I will do it with style rather than in a dull car."

"Ok, deal!"

We had a coffee before going through security.

"How are you going to get back to Munich?"

"Don't worry, I'll take the S-Bahn to the centre and then the U-Bahn or the tram. Maybe I will go for a walk in the city or have some tea with friends from the university. Will you call me when you arrive?"

"Count on it."

"I'm going to miss you."

She hugged me tight, ran her soft hand across my face and kissed me softly.

"Take care, Sophie."

"You too."

With that, I went through the security check and headed for the business lounge. I sat there, and for the first time in the last two days, I began processing what had just happened. I had no regrets. It was as if anything related to Sophie happened in a parallel universe where everything was different. There were no attachments to anything else. Everything was all right. Sophie was able to bring a combination of excitement, life, and quietness, all at the same time. All in the right proportions, as if it were the recipe of a delicious dish.

All my thoughts were interrupted by the beeping of my mobile, announcing the departure of my flight. I picked up my backpack and headed for the gate. I boarded the plane and spent the next two-and-a-half hours thinking about Sophie.

Sophie had become a part of my life, and now I was scared of whether I would be able to be at the level she deserved. How not to fall short? How not to screw this up? I didn't have a good record with people. I always managed to do the wrong thing at the wrong time. I never intended to do it, but acts are what counts, not the intentions. Time would just tell.

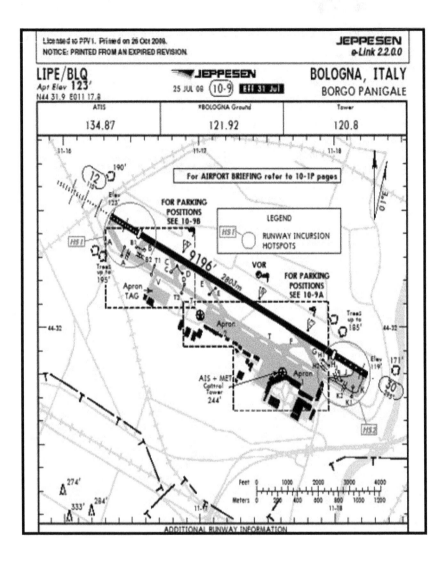

JEPPESEN
e-Link 2.2.0.0

LIPE/BLQ
Apt Elev **123'**
N44 31.9 E011 17.8

JEPPESEN
25 JUL 08 (10-9) Eff 31 Jul

BOLOGNA, ITALY
BORGO PANIGALE

ATIS	*BOLOGNA Ground	Tower
134.87	121.92	120.8

For AIRPORT BRIEFING refer to 10-1P pages

FOR PARKING POSITIONS SEE 10-9B

LEGEND

HS1 RUNWAY INCURSION HOTSPOTS

Elev 123'

12 190'

Trees up to 195'

Apron TAG

9196' 2803m

VOR

FOR PARKING POSITIONS SEE 10-9A

Trees up to 185'

Apron

44-32

Elev 119'

30 195'

AIS + MET
Control Tower 244'

Apron

171'

274'

284'

333'

Feet	0	1000	2000	3000	4000
Meters	0	200 400 600	800	1000	1200

ADDITIONAL RUNWAY INFORMATION

BLQ

BOLOGNA, ITALY

A fter those days in Munich, Sophie and I talked several times a day. Everyday. Day or night. Checking on each other, joking, sometimes more transcendental conversations, and sometimes just saying good morning, good night or just a random hi. I was still working for the same company working on different projects but without paying too much attention to them. My mind was on Sophie and everything else was just running on a parallel track, or behind, or not running at all. As Sophie would say, I was in shining mode more often than usual just to create more time so I could think about her. My brain seemed to really be working at 110 per cent. Anything work related was getting done at the speed of light. Everything was so easy to resolve, I even had time to help other people with their issues at work, with time to spare. Colleagues at work looked at me in disbelief. I was talkative, easy to reach, fun to be around. I was so active that every day after my morning shower, I had to write down all the ideas that were coming to my mind in those five minutes.

I guess I was just in love, or at minimum, I had a purpose to live for every day.

Sophie? Sophie? I was not so sure what she was doing. She seemed to always be doing something. She was always having something going on. Museums, music, friends, gym. In the distance, she seemed happy. I was always concerned the moment she would get alone and quiet in her apartment, because I could not understand the thoughts that would go through her head.

It turned out, I didn't have to wait too long to know. Two weeks after we saw each other, I got her call.

"Pack your things, Alvin!"

"Wait, what? Where am I going that I don't know about."

"Bologna, Italy."

"Bologna? When?"

"In two weeks."

"Huh, I will have to arrange some things."

"Sure, of course, you do. That's why I am giving you two weeks' notice. Otherwise, I would expect you there the following day!"

"Of course, you would. Yeah, let me work it out. I'll come back to you. Where are we staying?"

"Leave that to me, I will sort that out, but you'll take care of transportation."

"Flights and cars"

"Car. Flight. I'll get there on my own, and I'll meet you at the airport."

"Fine, as I said, let me sort things out tomorrow morning and then I will arrange the rest."

"Done!"

So, the next day I spent the time moving meetings around, cancelling visits, postponing others. Everything was getting done from the work point of view, but, truly, if the company had known what I was doing and how I was managing agendas, most probably I would have gotten fired. But, in a big company at a certain level, nobody cares how things are getting done as long as they get done, and the numbers turn green so people can have their bonuses.

In the evening, I called Sophie, and I told her that everything had been arranged for me to be in Italy as per her request. I was happy to go. Not only was I going to see Sophie and spend time with her, but it would also be a week of holidays. A week to relax. A week of holidays. I think both of us had been through a lot of stress. A stress that we ourselves had brought upon us.

Munich had been such a rush, and it was just on top of something that had been building between us for a while. It was not planned. I don't think anyone can plan for such a thing to happen, but it did happen, and now we both needed to manage this 'situation'.

Don't get me wrong, Sophie was great. Everything I could dream of, and more. I still had some questions about the heist in my head. In my head, that was difficult to accommodate. I don't know, maybe because I was raised in a very straight way. Not from a religious point of view, but with a clear understanding of what was right and what was not.

Depending on which side of the bed I would wake up on a day, I would think that what Sophie called a heist, it was not really that. Sophie claimed to get something that had no owner and that no one wanted it. Like picking up something in the middle of the street. So, maybe it was not so wrong after all. However, the breakage into the apartment was a little more difficult to reconcile for me. That was a property violation, and that in my book, was wrong.

In any case, I tried to fool myself into thinking that there was no violence. No one got hurt and something material can always be replaced. Or most of the time. Or maybe not. I would get into a conundrum which I refused to go into, as the last time I did I ended up in Zurich with a mental breakdown. I got scared there, and I didn't want to go back to that. Not sure if I would survive another night like that.

The next two weeks really went very slowly. I was looking forward to the escape to Italy so much that everything else just wouldn't catch my interest.

Finally, the day arrived, and I got to the airport for my flight. I think I smiled all the way to Bologna while looking through the window. As soon as I landed in Bologna, I started looking for Sophie at the airport. And there she was, reading something in one of the airport shops. I could only see her back but there was no way I would make a mistake. It was her. I coughed in a silly way; she turned around and gave me one of the longest and warmest hugs I ever got. Sophie broke her hug just to kiss me in a similar way. She was enjoying that feeling after three weeks of not seeing me in person. I also was in the same state and in the feeling mode. Recording her smell, her softness, her warmness, everything I could feel, all was being engraved in my brain.

"Hi, Alvin."

"Hi, Sophie."

"Did you have a good flight?"

"You know I love to fly, yes, it was great. You?"

"You know, just a short flight from Germany. Should we go?"

"Sure, let's get the luggage and the car, and we are all good to go."

I went to the rental car office. This time I accepted the upgraded car without hesitance.

"What did you get?"

"It is not a Jaguar! But it is still cool and glamorous."

I showed her the keys.

"An Alfa Romeo?"

"Well, this is Italy. The factory is not far from here, but cheer up, it is an Alfa Romeo Brera. Brand new, 10 km only. We will be the first. Let's check it out."

"Oh! It is not a Jaguar convertible, but it is a beautiful car."

"We will blend perfectly in the country with this one."

We placed the luggage in the trunk and jumped in.

"Ok. So, where to?"

"Via Cleto Tomba."

"Tomba as in the skier?"

"How on earth do you know that there is a skier named Tomba?"

"I just know. Look it up. It is true."

Sophie checked the fact on her phone while I was driving out of the airport. Driving in Italy is always challenging. Blinkers seemed to be an optional piece of equipment in most of the cars and driving outside of your lane is the standard. Thus, I needed all my senses. I really didn't want to trash a 50,000 Euros brand-new rental car. So, I focused on that. Sophie's hand on mine broke my attention, but I was getting used to her touch. Although I always strive to keep my personal space, I really enjoyed giving it up to Sophie.

"We have arrived, but I'm not seeing any hotel around. Are you sure of the address?"

"Sure I am. It is not a hotel. I got us an Airbnb. Much more private. Much more freedom."

"Yeah, sure. Why not? The building seems quite new, and I'm sure it will be nice."

Sophie was right. It was a nice, cosy apartment. A little bit similar to hers in Munich. Same style, but I guess all small apartments look alike. We settled in and Sophie prepared a small shopping list for food for the next days. We went back to the street and explored the area for a while. We did our shopping and went back to the apartment. We had dinner, and after that, we watched a movie.

I sat on the sofa and Sophie lay with her head on my lap. I ran my fingers through her hair, and she began to relax. I could feel her breathing slowing, almost matching mine. See, I'm a quiet man. My heartbeat is slow, my breathing is slow. Sophie's was quicker. Both her heartbeat and breathing were faster than mine. So, I could feel when she was relaxed, because she approached my cycles. Seeing her relaxed made me happy. It brought me a lot of calm. Maybe my body was not slowing further, but my head, my brain and my thoughts came to a freezing point, and that was my relaxing point.

Sophie slowly turned her head away from the TV and into my eyes. Those blue eyes were the only eyes I had been able to look straight into for more than two seconds. I could look into her eyes for minutes and scan their every single detail. Sophie would not take her eyes away as I think she knew that I loved that feeling. She smiled at me. I smiled back at her, and I kissed her softly, and then, well, you can guess what came next.

We woke up late next morning. This was a real holiday. No stress, no hurry, I had no plan for these days, but to spend time with Sophie and relax. Sophie on the other hand, most probably, would have a plan, all the things that she wanted to go and see. She would not randomly do things.

"So, what's the plan, Alvin?"

"I don't have a plan. I'm on vacation! You know well that I will disconnect my brain during these times."

"I know you do. Don't worry, I have you covered. Let's go to the city centre. There are a couple places I would like to check. We could also go to MamBo and the two towers and see the city from above."

"Works for me. Breakfast?"

"In a small 15 minutes' walk from here."

"Darn, you are so good."

As I said, she had a plan, and I could care less what she wanted to do, check, or go. I would be fine with it. I would just go along with her and enjoy the ride.

Sophie knew well that with an empty stomach, there was no way to get anything out of me. Not even a decent conversation. Thus, Sophie took me to the cafe she had selected, and I got myself a good breakfast.

"Now I feel like a person again. Where to?"

"Haha, it is incredible the miracles that coffee and some toast can perform on you, Alvin."

"I know I'm not very communicative before breakfast, but all good now."

"Then, let's go. I want to go to the MamBo and then to the towers."

"Sure, remind me again what is the MamBo. A dance? You know I have no rhythm whatsoever."

"Don't be silly. It is the Modern Art Museum Bologna—and yes, it is not a major flaw, but definitely, there is no rhythm in you."

We went to the museum and walked through the different rooms. I had never been to so many museums, art galleries and exhibitions in my whole life. Not that I didn't like them or had no interest in them, but I was always too busy or too lazy to go on my own. Sophie loved them. She couldn't get enough of them. I thought it was a good hobby to have.

In the afternoon, we went to the two towers and entered one of them. We climbed the stairs to the top of the tower. That was exhausting, but the views from the top of the tower were amazing. It was a sunny but chilly winter day. You could see the whole city and all the mountains around them.

"Great views, aren't they? It is unreal that they could build these towers so tall, so many years ago."

"Yes, they are."

"Do you see that mountain in front of us, Alvin?"

"Which one, the one with the castle on top?"

"Yes, that one. We are going there tomorrow."

"Oh, are we?"

"Yes, we'll take the car."

"You always have everything planned. I wonder what other things you have in mind for this trip."

"Haha, if only you knew."

We spent the rest of the day walking around the city. The Piazza Maggiore, the Basilica di San Petronio, La Piccola Venezia, and enjoyed all the small cafes and little shops around. It was getting dark, so we decided to go back to the apartment.

This time it was my turn to prepare something for dinner. Not that I have ever been a great cook. Day-to-day basic dishes. Only with desserts was I a little bit better, and only because I like sweet desserts after lunch. I managed to prepare a decent dinner for the both of us.

Sophie always appreciated being treated like a queen for a change. As much as I knew, she lived on her own. Definitely, she knew how to take care of herself, and needed no one to get around. That is for sure, but that also meant not having a minute to rest, and also having the discipline to not take the easy way out every time. She was disciplined, organised and strong. She would only show her vulnerability on limited occasions. Somehow, I was honoured that she showed that vulnerability to me. In return, I showed her true care. I could really see her enjoying the treat.

We had dinner and we sat on the sofa with the TV on.

"Tell me, how did we end up in Bologna? People come here for two things only. Buying packaging machines or attending university."

"Or a heist."

"Wait, what? You are kidding me. You can't possibly be serious about that."

"I'm always serious."

"Sophie! I thought we were here on holiday."

"And we are. Aren't we?"

"Yes, I mean. Yes."

"This is just like another activity on our holiday. Like an outdoor activity, just to have something different from the museums and the normal, every-tourist plans."

"A heist is not 'a recreational activity', Sophie. Going to the park, driving go-karts or even paintball can be, but a heist? I thought the Munich thing was a one-off. Something, that for whatever reason you wanted, or had to do. I trusted you, and I agreed on the basis that it was just that time."

"You agreed with yourself on just the one-time thing. I never mentioned that, and you never mentioned to me those were the conditions."

"No, I didn't. You are right. That's beyond the point."

I paused for a minute so I could reprocess the whole situation but really couldn't make too much sense out of it.

"But how?"

"Same modus operandi as Munich. Get in, get out, ten minutes, no violence."

"With the exception that you know Munich well. You have been living there at times for a while. What do you know of Bologna? Is there going to be another open apartment? Where? How? When?"

"Relax, I have everything under control."

"I'm sorry, Sophie, but it is difficult to relax with all these unknowns."

"The house is empty. It is outside of the old walls of the city, so traffic should be a problem. This time we will escape away from the city centre, unlike Munich. To the mountain I showed you in the morning when we were at the top of the tower."

"Have you been here before? How do you know which apartment? When did you plan all this? Was it before Munich or after? Did you plan this for me all along? What are we going for this time? Jewellery? A painting?"

"Alvin, one question at the time. No, I've never been to Bologna before, but I have my contacts. The information is good. It will not be a problem. I know which house, which floor, which apartment. I planned this after Munich. I couldn't plan it before that. I couldn't tell if you would agree on the Munich thing, first of all. A small piece of jewellery, as I said. Same thing."

"But why? Why do this? Why take any risk for a small piece of jewellery? Is it about money? Because you don't need to. I have enough money for both of us. I thought Munich was maybe about a family issue, a former boyfriend or whatever, but now?"

"I don't need your money, Alvin. I have never needed anyone's, and I don't need yours."

"I'm sorry, I didn't want to imply that…"

"I know you didn't. Look, it will be like Munich and then we can continue. Everything will be alright."

I stared out the window. Sophie came to me from behind and hugged me. I looked down, and I felt trapped, as if I was left with no choice.

"Do you have a map? I would like to make sure I can drive us out of this one."

I turned around and Sophie gave me that small smile of hers.

"Of course, I do. This time, no practice run needed. Just turn right and we are in the Autostrada. The destination at the mountain's top is easy to set in the car's GPS."

"Alright, it seems simple enough."

"I told you, easy-peasy."

"What am I going to do with you, Sophie?"

She didn't answer. She just kissed me, and with that, all my defences were gone. We spent the rest of the night reviewing Sophie's plan.

Next morning, I woke up earlier. Two seconds after I reached the conscious state, reality hit me again. This heist thing was really getting into my head. I was feeling more and more uncomfortable with it while I was getting more and more comfortable with Sophie. I guess I was thinking too loud, as Sophie began to wake up as well. She turned around in bed and looked me in the eyes. Man, I can still close my eyes and see hers.

"Hey."

"Hey."

"Come on, let's have breakfast and get going with our outdoor activity."

"Really, Sophie. 'Our outdoor activity', you crack me up."

"Oh, come on. It will be ten minutes of waiting and then we can get to the mountain for the rest of the day. Look, it is sunny, I'm sure it will be sunny up there as well."

We left the apartment and took the car. We drove to the west of the city, to an I that Sophie had chosen. We had a quick breakfast without talking too much.

"It is time, let's go, Alvin."

I finished my coffee and paid the bill. I followed Sophie's instructions to a wide street. I parked where she guided me. As she said, next to the Autostrada. It will be an easy way out.

"One more minute, and I will go."

"Ok."

"Alvin?"

"Yes."

"Thanks for being here with me, for me."

She kissed me and got out of the car.

"Ten minutes, and I'll be back. Keep it running."

"Right."

As usual, every time I was under stress, worried, mad or just hungry, my conversation would be reduced to monosyllables. In this case, it was a combination of stress, worry and being mad. This was a different sensation from the one I had in Munich. My heartbeat was going faster than a racehorse, and I was breathing fast.

I watch all the car's mirrors checking for people, police, anything that could put an end to this madness. It also crossed through my mind, the idea of driving away and leaving Sophie right there, but I couldn't. How could I do that?

All my thoughts were interrupted by the slam of the car door.

"Go."

"Uh?"

"Go, Alvin! Go!"

I switched into gear and floored the gas pedal. I turned right as was planned and made the car fly through the highway. 130, 150, 170 km/h. Pretty soon, we were at the exit to the mountain. I drove to the top of the hill as fast as the road and the car allowed me. I had to burn some steam somehow. I reached the top of the mountain and stopped at a lookout area. I got out of the car, slamming the door, and walked to the edge of the lookout and stood there.

Sophie was still in the car. She was smart enough to let me be alone for a while. She knew me well, and she knew I was quite slow with feelings. Pushing me without letting me go through them, it would be a mistake she would regret. I mean, not that I have ever gotten aggressive with anyone, and for sure, I wouldn't get aggressive with anyone, and even less with Sophie.

She let me be there alone for 15 minutes. In those 15 minutes, I thought about how I ended up with something I loved and hated. How two diametrically opposed things were pulling me apart. I had Sophie who I genuinely loved by now, and I had this heist thing that I couldn't live with. It was Zurich's nightmare all over again. I could not pretend that there were no consequences. Losing her or losing my head. Me without my head is a worthless thing to have. I had to be right with me before I could be right for anyone else. The heist thing made me wrong and therefore I couldn't be right for Sophie.

Sophie stepped out of the car and slowly got closer to me. She knew this was not a joke for me, so she wouldn't play any joke in this situation. She didn't touch me.

"Are you alright, Alvin?"

"No, Sophie, I am not. I can't do this anymore."

"What do you mean?"

"The heists. I can't do them anymore. I'm not ok with that. I can't fit them into my head.""What do you mean?"

"I can't fit them into my head. Not from the legal, social, behavioural, or however you want to call it, and I cannot fit them from the logical point of view in my head."

"I understand."

"I don't think you do. Sophie, there is no such thing as a perfect heist or robbery. Sooner or later, something goes wrong. For fuck's sakes, even in the movies they go wrong, and they write the argument."

"I will never be caught."

"Sophie, you are smart. One of the smartest people I have crossed paths with in my life, but do not overestimate yourself. Mistakes are made, and they are not planned."

"No mistakes with this, Alvin."

"What is that even supposed to mean?"

"You are not a mistake."

"I need time to process this, Sophie. I can't work this out right here, right now. I just can't."

"It is ok."

"You know I love you."

"I love you too."

We hugged. The kind of hug that you give when you know someone is struggling with something, and you try to let them know that they are not alone. I broke down. We both did. We both had tears in our eyes. We both cared so much for each other that we knew what this conversation meant for us.

"Let's go home, Sophie."

"Yes, let's go home."

We both got in the car, and I slowly drove out of the lookout. I drove at a slow pace all the way to the apartment. Sophie held my hand, and it looked as if she didn't want to let me go. I was afraid. I was afraid that the moment we would get out of the car we would lose each other forever, and that the frame of the car would keep us safe and as one.

In the apartment, we didn't speak too much but there was a mood of love. Every opportunity we had we touched one another, we used it wisely, slowly, making sure that we would remember it.

We lay on the sofa and watched TV. I ran my fingers through her thin hair again and again. Not talking. Just touching and feeling. She looked up to me, and I did a slow gentle massage on her face. Her forehead, her cheeks, her lips, her neck, her nose her ears, her eyes. I have her whole face scanned into my head, and I can bring that up in my head again and again.

The next day, we packed our things and went to the airport. We made it just in time to catch our flights. We looked at the departure screens and looked at each other and hugged.

"Sophie, please take care. Please."

"I will, Alvin. You take care too."

We split apart, and I looked at her one last time as she boarded her gate with her head down. I boarded mine, and I silently cried throughout the flight.

The next weeks, we tried to keep in contact, but nothing was the same. We both tried to avoid the main questions. That situation only brought more stress and more pain to an already difficult mental situation. A situation that only required acceptance on my side, but about which I could not make a decision.

I knew I could not have it both ways, but I also knew I had to put an end to the situation one way or another. This was weighing too much on me, and I was quite sure it was doing the same on Sophie's side. It was not fair to her to keep her waiting. She had to move on with or without me. I also needed to make a decision for myself, even if it was not the one I wanted.

Somehow, I found the courage to call her one night.

"Hey, Sophie."

"Hey, Alvin."

"How are you?"

"I'm doing alright, you?"

"Look, I just want to talk to you. I can't do it."

"It is your decision, Alvin."

"I know it is, but this can't keep going like this, we are hurting too much."

"Yes, it hurts. A lot. More than you can possibly imagine."

"I think I do because it hurts here as well."

"But you're still doing it, and I do not understand it."

"I can't explain it."

"It is ok, Alvin. Take care. Bye-bye, Alvin."

"Bye, Sophie."

We hung up the line and we both cried. I couldn't see Sophie, but I know she did. I cried and then I was myself for a while. Actually, I don't think I have ever been the same again. I have never been with anyone afterwards. Sophie set the bar too high for anyone to get there.

After a while, I tried to see how she was doing. I know she wouldn't contact me again, but the care I had for her has never faded.

Suddenly the announcement of the gate brought me back to the current space and time. I was still in Keflavik telling the story to the private investigator I had hired to find Sophie.

"So yes, that was the story behind Sophie."

"I see. That is not an everyday story."

"No, it is not. Sophie is not an everyday woman, but the search is over. I cannot keep going on like this. It is time to turn the page."

"You will never be able to do that. You know that, don't you?"

"I have to."

"You won't. You can't. You'll keep searching, and it will be a matter of time before we meet again. For what I don't know, you won't turn the page, although you will pretend that you have, and you will even be able to fool most people, but anyone who knows the story—and knows you—knows this will not happen."

"In any way, your case is over. You are dismissed."

"For now."

"Thanks for the work."

"Thanks for the money and the trips. I would have never come to Iceland if it weren't for you."

We shook hands, and we both boarded our flights.

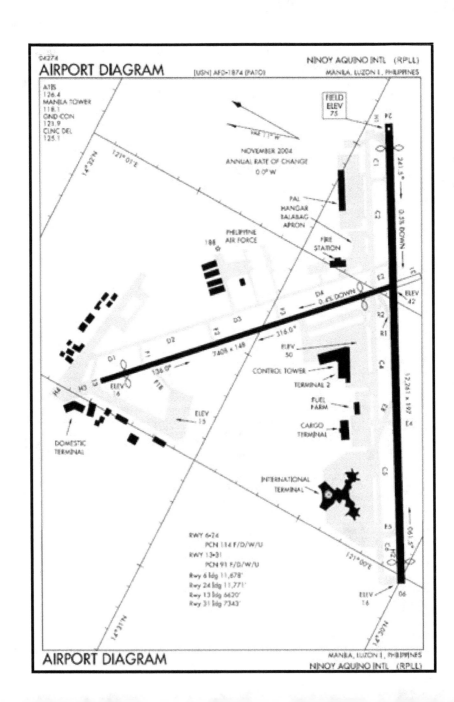

MNL

MANILA, PHILIPPINES

Iceland had put an end to my hopes. More than a year had gone by. I was feeling depressed, sad and empty. Still, I couldn't get Sophie out of my head, and I thought about her every single day. Most probably, that did not help the situation. On any other occasion, I would have thrown myself into work just to keep my head busy, but I could care less about work. Work was just a place to go for eight or nine hours a day. I wasn't doing too much, and eventually, that got me into some trouble.

Some brilliant mind had the idea of sending me on a tour around Europe to visit plants and suppliers to find ideas and opportunities. I was not very keen on doing that either, but I was left with no choice. So, I accepted it. I decided I would consider it a week of holidays. I thought that maybe travelling a little bit would relax me, or at the very minimum, it would put my head somewhere else. The one-week trip would take me to the usual places. Germany, Italy, Belgium and Switzerland.

The very moment I sat on the aeroplane and the door was closed, I realised that the trip was going to become hell. A lot of the memories and places I had made and been with Sophie were going to be revisited, and I was not ready for that. The rational part of my brain tried to tell me that, maybe, confronting pain would help to overcome my fears, that, maybe, and only maybe, if I was able to make it through that trip, I would prevail.

The trip really went from bad to worse as I was moving countries. By the time I got to Milan on a Wednesday, I could barely hold my tears inside, and I wasn't even in Bologna. I don't think I could step into that city anymore. Too many memories. I made it to the end of the week just because I didn't have a choice.

The following week I took some time off to think about what to do. I could not keep going like this for too much longer and if I did, I was not sure how I would end up. The idea of changing my life radically was gaining more and more weight. A different company, different city, country or continent. It was not an endeavour to take lightly. I had lived in different countries in the past, and I was aware of the complexity of these changes. Still, I thought that no matter the complexity, anything would be better than keeping the situation as it was. So, I decided to at least do the exercise.

Changing company was always an option and most probably would bring an additional change of location, but the uncertainties of a new job could add too much stress. Staying in my current company was the easiest but where to go? Europe? That was out of the question. I would not stick around because it would be matter of time, and I would end up in the same places all over again. North America? I had lived there already for six years. I could make it there, but I didn't stay at the time and although circumstances had changed, something told me that it wouldn't last. South America? Africa? The Middle East? I just couldn't picture myself there. Australia? Too far away. I was running out of options, and I was feeling stuck again.

I was sleeping through another boring Tuesday at the office when I was pinged on the Lync. I had no clue who it was. It didn't sound familiar to me, but again, in a big company, it is difficult to know everyone. He wanted to set up a call with me to talk about a position open for an engineer in another region. It is always easier when people come to you with opportunities than trying to find them yourself, so I agreed to have a discussion. There was nothing to lose and maybe something to help me keep going with my life.

The discussion ended up being a full interview with senior management from the other region. The Philippines? Well, that one was most definitely not on my radar, but the company would pay for relocation, trips and arrangements. So, it seemed like a good deal to me. The work could not be that difficult anyway. I knew the product and the machines.

Nothing to be worried about. I accepted the offer. Money was not much, but it wasn't the main driver anyway. I packed up and got ready to move on.

The flight to Manila through Dubai was a pleasant one, especially when your flight was business class. For the first time in a long time, I felt a little bit of a break. Sophie was still in my head but at least I had some resemblance of control and direction for my life, or so I thought.

I landed in Manila on 21 November at around nine at night. The airport seemed to be okay. Clean, modern and cold. The air conditioning might be set below 20 degrees. Too cold for my taste. I went through passport control, picked up my luggage and left the security area. A young man was waiting for me holding a screen with my name.

"Hello, I'm Alvin."

"Hello Sir, I am Wilmer. I will take you to the hotel now. Let me take your luggage."

"I'll take the blue one, you can take the grey one. Thank you."

The automatic door of the airport opened, and I got hit by a rush of hot and humid air. For a second, I just could not breathe. I was gasping for some fresh air. I turned my head around, I put it back inside the airport building where the air was cold, and I took a deep breath. I tried to make it to the car, but I ran short, and the hot and humid air hit me again. I got enough air somehow, to take the luggage in the trunk of the car and jump inside. The temperature inside the car was freezing again.

Wilmer got in and started the car.

"Sorry Wilmer, what is the temperature outside?"

"30 degrees, Sir."

"And what time is it now?"

"It is ten at night, Sir."

"Ten at night, 30 degrees at the end of November. Is this the standard?"

"Sure thing, Sir."

"And don't call me Sir. I am Alvin."

"Sure thing."

After a long drive, we arrived at the hotel. I was surprised to have a security check in the car before reaching the main front door. There were dogs, metal detectors and mirrors to check below the car. Every car had to open its trunk, and the dogs would sniff everything.

"Is this the standard?"

"Yes, it is, since we had a terrorist attack five years ago."

I couldn't even remember that attack and then I realised how far Manila was from Europe. I checked in and was taken to my room in the hotel. It was a very luxurious hotel. One of the best, once I checked all the reviews. Once again, the room was freezing. I thought that this air conditioning thing was going to become a theme in the Philippines for me.

I slept well that night. Maybe because of the 18-hour trip, and maybe because of jet lag, I was hungry. I took a shower and went downstairs for breakfast. This time around it was an 'intercontinental' breakfast. I went for food at least three times if not four. I checked my mobile and checked the weather: 29 degrees at seven in the morning. It was hilarious seeing people wearing light jackets, because obviously in the morning it is always a little bit fresher. I finished my breakfast and went to the reception of the hotel with the idea of hiring a car to move around. To my surprise, Wilmer was there waiting for me.

"Good morning, Sir."

"Good morning, Wilmer. What are you doing here? Are you picking up someone else?"

"No, Sir."

"No, Alvin."

"Yes, Sir, I am here to pick you up."

"Actually, I was going to hire a car."

"No car for you, Sir. The company thinks it is safer for you if I drive you around for now. I think it is safer for you if I drive you around."

"Nonsense. I have been driving cars in every country I have been to."

"Not here, or at least not for now. Let me take you to work."

"Ok, I'm not going to argue with you."

"Shall we go then?"

"Yes, Wilmer, let's go."

I jumped into the car and Wilmer began to drive around the hotel. As soon as we got out to the hotel square, I understood right away. There were no clear traffic lines. The number of lines was determined by the width of the road divided by the width of the cars. Whatever number that would be. The highway, called Skyway, wasn't any better, and that was the best road around, as it had a toll.

"Tell me, Wilmer, is it always like this?"

"Yes, Sir. Now it is a little bit worse, as it is rush hour, and everyone tries to get to work on time."

"How far is the plant?"

"Oh, around one hour away."

I was looking through the window, and I saw and experienced a completely different landscape. Life was on the street. Literally. People were cooking and having lunch on the street. Some women were washing their clothes on the street, a man was pulling a full engine out of a car on the street, and children were playing on the street. I wasn't even sure if there was anything beyond the first row of houses that I could see from the car.

We arrived at the factory. Everything seemed quite organised on this side of the fence. Like an oasis in the middle of general disorganisation. I was taken to my office and once I set up my gear, I was offered a plant tour by the plant manager and one of the engineers. I was very keen to check my new workplace, where I could put my brain to work and get busy with other things, so I was not thinking about Sophie. They guided me out of the office and into the manufacturing area. There was a security guard with a metal detecting wand and a full detection arch similar to the ones in the airport.

"What is all this about?"

"What do you mean, the security and the metal detection check?"

"Yes, that."

"In the past we had people taking some metal parts home. I guess they could find a different use somewhere for them. Last time that happened, someone took a part of the formats, and we had to stop the line for a month until we could get a replacement from Europe. Paying the security guard is cheaper than stopping the line."

"Ah, ok, I see. I have never seen this before."

"You were never here before."

"True."

I began to work on the projects that I had been assigned. Nothing of this was new to me, and I soon found myself comfortable working with the people in the plant. They were all very polite, and to tell the truth, quite professional and good at their work.

After the first three or four weeks, the rush of having to live in a new country, in a new culture, with new people was starting to fade away. At the end of the day, I had spent all my life working with people from diverse backgrounds, in different countries, so this should not be any different. Except for the unbearable weather with humid and hot days and the air conditioning hell, everything was according to plan and as I had expected it to be. As I was settling in from the physical point of view, I began to feel more unsettled from the emotional point of view. Weekdays were more or less tolerable as I would be working long hours, but weekends started to become more and more difficult to bear with.

Sophie was in my head every day but now she was becoming increasingly present. I just couldn't find enough things to do to keep my brain busy. I couldn't force myself to do something I was not motivated to do, or learn, because I would last ten minutes on it.

I thought maybe going somewhere else would ease the gears in my head. Although it was early, I called Wilmer and asked him to pick me up.

"Hi, Wilmer, sorry to call you on a Saturday."

"No sorry, Sir, my job is to drive you around whenever you need to."

"I know, but it is Saturday, and it should be your day off, right?"

"It is ok, Sir. Where to?"

"Take me to a museum."

"A museum? Which one?"

"Anyone."

"Uh, ok."

Wilmer drove as I looked through the window without having a clue where I was or where I was going. It was always difficult for me to get references in such a large city.

"We have arrived, Sir."

"Where are we?"

"Fort Santiago. From here you can visit the old fort and walk to Intramuros, the old city. It is full of small museums and churches. If you walk a little bit further, you will get to Rizal Park. There are at least four museums close to each other. I think this will be enough."

"Yes, Wilmer, I think it will be enough. Thank you."

"Any time, Sir."

I spent the rest of the Saturday walking through the places Wilmer had suggested to me. Museums were big and quiet. Somehow, that forced my brain to a quiet mode as well. As if my thoughts would be able to disturb the silence of the rooms. I pretended sometimes that Sophie was there as well, just one step behind me. But she wasn't.

The museums began to close one by one. I walked to the fort next to the beach and sat there to watch one of the most beautiful sunsets I had ever seen. I stayed there until the sun went down and the night came up. I didn't really want to call Wilmer, but I was not feeling very safe in that part of the town alone at night. So, I did.

"Where to, Sir? The hotel?"

"I don't really feel like going to the hotel, to be honest. Where do people go on a Saturday night?"

"Rich people would go to the pub in the city centre close to the hotel."

"I'm not that kind of person. What do normal people do? Where would you go on a night like this?"

"I would go to one of the bar-restaurants on the way to work."

"Take me to one of those."

"I'll take you to a place I go with friends. Some of them may be there."

"Go for it."

That or anything else that wasn't the hotel would have worked for me that night. We arrived at a place full of people. As Wilmer said it was a combination of a restaurant and a bar. Lots of people were eating traditional dishes while having Spanish heritage beers. It turned out to be a good place to go as I was starving. We sat at a big table.

"Order something to eat and some beers. I'll take care of the bill."

Pretty soon the whole table was full of dishes and a bucket of ice and beers. Wilmer and I began to talk until some of his friends came along. Suddenly, there were around 20 people sitting at the table. All of them were good friends of Wilmer. It always surprises me when people have a lot of friends. I could count mine with one hand, and I will not use half of the fingers.

It was almost impossible for me to follow the conversations as people would switch between English and Tagalog all the time. Tagalog was the local language which was a combination of the Indigenous language, Spanish and English. Still, I was having a wonderful time with Wilmer and his friends.

We stayed there until past midnight. By that time, I had had enough beers, and I was ready to be taken home. Some people would stay longer, but I just had enough. Wilmer took me back to the hotel and once we passed the hotel security, he asked,

"Well, Sir, have a good night. Will you need me tomorrow?"

"Thank you, Wilmer. No, I don't think I will be able to go anywhere tomorrow. It has been a great night. I needed it. Too many beers, maybe."

"Yes, it happens sometimes. Take care, Sir."

I went to my room and somehow, I made it to bed. I don't think I fell asleep; I think I just fell unconscious.

I woke up the next day with a hangover. It had been a long time since the last one, as I would not drink on a regular basis. Sunday morning passed very slowly. By midday, I had begun to recover some of my brain cells' functionality. Alcohol seemed to have erased Sophie out of my brain for a while. However, I knew that wasn't the solution. Alcohol has never been a solution for anything in my life and now would be no different. Drugs? I have never ever taken any at all, and I was not going to start now.

As the day progressed, I started questioning myself if this decision to move to the Philippines was the best one for me to take. Coming from a small tidy quiet town to a big crowded and chaotic city like Manila, maybe it was too much of a change for me. The weather, the noise, the crowds—it was so different from what I knew. I couldn't find anything to look at, that wasn't blocked by a street or by a building. I was used to living in a place where I could look out the window and find empty fields or mountains in the distance. The only place I could do that in Manila was by going to the seafront. Not being able to manage myself with my own transportation was also not helping, but, in reality, driving in the traffic chaos would have been challenging, to say the least.

Somehow, now I was trapped in an unusual way. I had a commitment to the company and if I wanted to break it, it would cost me money, and that was fair. However, money had never been a motivation for me. I wouldn't take a job just because of the money, and I wouldn't stop doing something for money, as long as I could afford it. I was feeling more for the people at work. I really enjoyed working with them.

I decided to give myself two more weeks to see if I could make the situation work, but I had low confidence in it, yet I still tried. However, dealing with Sophie in my head, and with the day-to-day, proved to be too much for me. So, I took the decision to leave. I asked for a meeting with the management and agreed to pay back some of the relocation costs. The question was where to go from here. I couldn't go back to Europe so I thought I could go only further away. South. Maybe Australia? New Zealand? I would explore what I could do there, and I would repack again if I was unable to get a job.

In the meantime, I decided to take some holidays to reorganise my brain and try to set up the nth plan. I called Wilmer.

"Wilmer?"

"Yes, Sir."

"I need a last ride to the airport."

"To the airport?"

"Yes, I'm leaving the country."

"Oh, that is too bad. I'll be at the hotel in 15 minutes."

"Thanks."

I checked out of the hotel which had been my home for the last three months and took my luggage to the entrance until Wilmer showed up.

"Hello, Sir. Let me get your luggage."

"Thanks, Wilmer, let's go."

"To the airport."

"Yes, to the Airport, but don't take the Skyway. Drive me through the neighbourhoods. Drive slowly. Turn the air conditioning off and open the windows."

"How much time do we have to get to the airport, Sir?"

"About seven hours, we have time."

I let Wilmer drive me around, through the various parts of the city. The nice ones, the rich ones, the middle-class ones and the poor ones. Somehow, Wilmer understood what I wanted, and he drove me to the Fort. He stopped the car, and I stepped out. I went to the waterfront and looked one last time at the sunset over the ocean. Wilmer waited patiently for me to come back to the car.

"Thank you, Wilmer, I think I am good to go now."

"No problem, Sir. Yes, I think now you are ok to go."

Wilmer drove to the airport and got my luggage out.

"Thank you again, Wilmer. Thank you for driving me everywhere and for taking me to your friends. I have really enjoyed being here."

"No problem, Sir."

"Here I got you a small farewell present, it is not a big thing but…"

"Sir, I don't have any present for you."

"You gave it to me at the Fort already."

"Thank you, Sir. It has been my pleasure."

I shook hands with him and gave him a hug. I took my luggage, and I headed to the airport entrance. As I was going to enter the building, I heard Wilmer.

"Hey!"

"Yes?"

"Good Luck, Alvin!"

Somehow at that moment, I realised that the relationship with Wilmer had changed from a professional one to a friendship. To this day,

I have still kept in contact with him. Some of the people at work as well, like Noel, Stevenson, Rommel, and some others.

I sat in the business class lounge, and I thought that if it wasn't for Sophie, I would have never come to the Philippines, and I would have never met all these great people. Sophie had pushed me to do a lot of things, and somehow, her influence was still pushing me to do new ones. I was just trying to convince myself, that out of all the sadness that I had around my memories with her, at least I was growing somehow in a positive way.

All my thoughts were interrupted once again by the gate announcement. I finished my coffee, grabbed my gear and headed to the gate. Another airport, another flight, another destination. This time more uncertain than ever, but I think certainty was becoming a luxury I could not afford anymore.

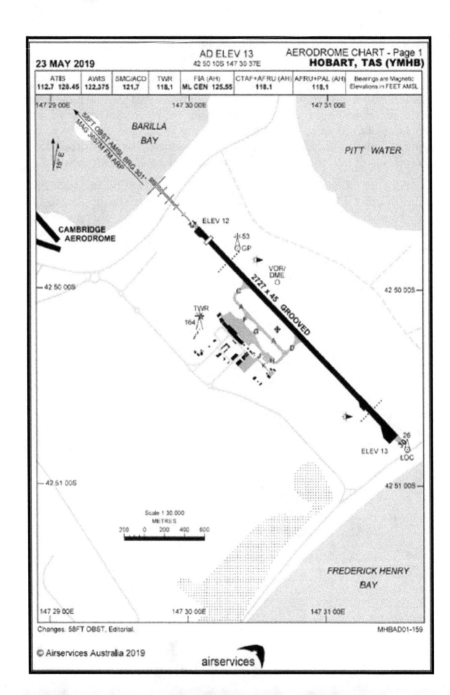

| ATIS 112.7 128.45 | AWIS 122.375 | SMC/ACD 121.7 | TWR 118.1 | FIA (AH) ML CEN 125.55 | CTAF+AFRU (AH) 118.1 | AFRU+PAL (AH) 118.1 | Bearings are Magnetic Elevations in FEET AMSL |

147 29 00E

147 30 00E

147 31 00E

BARILLA BAY

PITT WATER

58FT OBST AMSL BRG 301°
MAG 385TM FM ARP

16° E

ELEV 12

CAMBRIDGE AERODROME

53
GP

VOR/DME

42 50 00S

42 50 00S

2727 x 45 GROOVED

TWR
164

42 51 00S

26
301
ELEV 13
LOC

Scale 1 30 000
METRES
200   0   200   400   600

FREDERICK HENRY BAY

147 29 00E

147 30 00E

147 31 00E

Changes: 58FT OBST, Editorial.

MHBAD01-159

airservices

HBA

HOBART, AUSTRALIA

The plane landed hard on the runway. I looked outside the airplane door waiting my turn to disembark. It was a miserable, windy and rainy day, and I thought to myself, "What on earth am I doing here?" I got into the terminal. Welcome to Hobart. Well, the weather didn't support the welcome at all.

As I had done hundreds of times before in other airports around the world, I followed the routine of getting my luggage, picking up my rental car and driving to the hotel. I chose a hotel by the waterfront, and the views from the hotel room did not disappoint. I had a magnificent view of the port area, and through the mist, I could see a big cruise ship docked in the port. I thought that on a clear sunny day, the sight had to be magnificent.

I sighed, took my mobile and thought that it was time for me to get done with the purpose of my trip to Tasmania.

"Dr Johnstone speaking?"

"Uh, yes, hello, Dr Karen Johnstone?"

"Yes, it is me."

"Hello. My name is Alvin, I would like to make an appointment."

"Is this for yourself?"

"Yes, it is for me."

"Sure, no worries. I can book you in tomorrow at ten in the morning if it works for you."

"Yes, ten o'clock is fine."

"Perfect, I need you to fill in a form with basic information about yourself. Please, would you be able to send it before today at five? Do you think you could manage?"

"Yes, yes. Send it to me, and I will get it done right away."

"You can find the form on my webpage. Simply basic information."

"Sure, no problem."

"Ok, I will see you tomorrow at ten then."

"Yes, thank you."

I connected my laptop and filled in the form as requested. I held my finger above the mouse bottom for the longest time. I was not sure if there was going to be any use to this new approach at all, but I haven't been feeling myself lately. Actually, I had not been feeling myself since I left Bologna and Sophie, and I could admit that I was getting worse with time, not better. Finally, I clicked, and I sent the form. I needed to help myself as no one else would do it for me.

I spent the rest of the day relaxing at the hotel. A little bit at the swimming pool, a little bit at the spa. However, it seemed that my body and my brain were completely disconnected. My body was relaxed. I breathed slowly, my heartbeat was slow, I ate and slept well, but my brain was in a non-stop mode.

The next morning, I had a mixed feeling between the desire to cancel everything and run away and the wish to get some peace in my brain. Finally, I decided to leave the hotel room and walk to my appointment. I needed to get through this, and I felt I wouldn't be able to do it without help.

"Hello, Alvin. Please come in."

"Hello, Dr Johnstone, thank you."

"Karen, please. Call me Karen. Please take a seat, feel comfortable."

"Thank you."

"Ok, let's start. A couple of ground rules for this session. This is an initial session. After this session today, I will make a decision if I think I can help you, or if I am not the help you need. Second, for this session or future ones, if that would be the case, the success of this process lies on you. Be honest. There is no point in lying to me. That doesn't help you, and it doesn't help me."

"I am clear. Fair enough."

"Well, let's start. Why are you here?"

"I'm trying to get some help."

"What do you need help with?"

"Trying to deal with the loss of a person."

"Is that person dead?"

"No, she is not, or at least I really hope she is not dead. Hopefully, she is well."

"What's her name?"

"Sophie."

"Why don't you tell me about Sophie?"I laid back on the chair, then I looked down.

"Yes. I mean yes, I will tell you about Sophie."

I spent the next 45 minutes telling my story about Sophie. Karen just sat there without interrupting me. Just listening carefully and taking notes.

"…and that is my story with Sophie."

"Thank you, Alvin. Let me ask you. Have you used a psychologist's service before?"

"Yes, I have. I tried twice."

"Tried?"

"First time I was there for one session. The second time with a different doctor, I lasted two sessions."

"Did you decide to stop the sessions, or did the professionals decide they could not help you?"

"I was the one stopping the sessions."

"How come?"

"I had the feeling that I was coming to conclusions faster than they were."

"I see. So, you were assuming that the final conclusions that the professionals would be able to reach would be similar to the ones you already had in your head."

"Something like that."

"Then, why are you here? Why do you think this time will be different?"

"I don't know. Time has passed. Maybe, before everything was too fresh and now everything is more settled in my head."

"I see. Alvin, I have been looking into you before this session. You have an impressive professional curriculum. You seem like a pretty smart person."

"Maybe I fooled everyone."

"Did you? Why would you?"

"I don't know, what do you think?"

"Alvin, this session is about what you feel and think, not about me. What I believe or think is irrelevant. Alvin, smart, qualified people work in a completely unique way. Their brain is wired in a certain manner, and often, they tackle problems in the same way that they would a problem at their profession."

"What do you mean by that?"

"Have you ever analysed your feelings with Sophie as you would with an issue at work? You are an engineer, right?"

"Yes, I am."

"Have you ever written on a piece of paper or on a computer, a root cause analysis, five whys, or a flow diagram of your feelings for Sophie?"

I looked down again as if I had been caught red-handed.

"...yes, I have."

"And you couldn't solve it or get it to a conclusion, right?"

"If I had, maybe I wouldn't be here, right?"

"Yes, I guess you wouldn't. Ok, time is up for today. Let's schedule another session for tomorrow."

"Does that mean that you take my case?"

"Case? This is not a police investigation, but yes. I will try to help you."

"Why?"

"When you were working on a project, did you like an innovative design project or a project where the solution you could get off the shelf was better?"

"An innovative design is always more challenging."

"The more complex the person, the more challenging it is. We psychologists are not different from engineers. Tomorrow, same time."

"Ok, I'll be here. Thank you, Karen."

"Thank you, Alvin."

I left the office and went for a walk. I wasn't sure how I was feeling. Telling my story about Sophie was never easy, as a lot of feelings were involved in it, but there was no other way to do it. All my feelings for Sophie, before and after we took different paths, had never been shared with anyone except my two previous attempts with psychologists. It would have been difficult to explain to people I knew that I had been involved in two heists. Most probably, everyone would have looked at me and said, "That's a funny joke. Alvin participating in heists. Yeah right. Sure." No one would have believed me.

The next morning, I really didn't want to get out of bed. Even less, to go and talk to anyone. Still, I did my best and walked myself to the psychologist's office.

"Good morning, Alvin. I wasn't sure if you would come for this second appointment."

"Barely, good morning."

"Please take a seat. How are you today?"

"Doing fine."

"Why are you here today?"

"I guess it is the same reason as yesterday…"

"Right. Tell me something, Alvin, would you describe yourself as an honest person?"

I try to be honest, but, no, I am not an honest person. I am not honest with others, and I am not honest with myself. It is funny when you think about it, because a person being honest about his dishonesty may be the most honest thing he might say."

"Well, that is definitely a remarkably interesting word game you put together. Does it bother you?"

"Not being honest? Of course, it does bother me. If it wouldn't I would just be a jackass."

"So, why be dishonest?"

"Let me ask you something, do you think the human race could make it without lies?"

"We have been through this already, Alvin. This is not about what I think, so what do you think? Do you think humanity would be able to make it without lies?"

"No, I don't think so."

"Why so?"

"I don't think people are ready to handle truths and that includes me as well. We will end up killing each other or not talking to each other and therefore no civilisation. We lie to protect others and to protect ourselves. Humans cannot be honest all the time"

"I see. In your form, you mentioned you are an engineer. Tell me about your job a little bit. What do you actually do?"

"I work as a project engineer. I get assigned projects or problems, and I try to figure them out. That's what I get paid for in general."

"Tell me about the projecting part."

"Well, as its name says it is a projection of the present into the future or vice versa."

"So, there is some level of guessing on it."

"Well, that's what the engineering part comes in. You project based on your data, or the parameters, or the information you have."

"But you have to make a lot of assumptions."

"Yes. I do. There is always an unknown part for which you don't have data, or the data is so complex that it is impossible to analyse. So, yes, I predict, estimate, guess what the future would look like based on the data that I have, or I try to interpret a future idea in the present. That's what a project engineer should do, or at least that's what I think."

"Do you do the same with people?"

"I'm not sure I understand. What do you mean?"

"Do you project people's reactions? Do you assume what other people's actions, feelings, thoughts will be?"

"There is no way to predict or project that. No one can."

"But you try, and I really believe that you try to do it for the right reasons. I believe you are not trying to take advantage of that, just trying to do what you think is right and best for you and other people. However, by assuming someone else's decision you are taking that chance from them. You cannot and should not decide on behalf of other people even if your intentions are good."

"I know that. I guess I have an issue with overthinking sometimes, in some cases."

"Is this overthinking happening with everything or just Sophie?"

"Mainly with people, especially with Sophie."

"Is this why you are here?"

"Is this going to be a recurrent question?"

"Yes, until you are ready to give me a full answer on it. Anyway, time is up. I'll see you tomorrow at the same time."

So far Karen was really drilling me in the right direction. However, she had not hit me with anything I didn't know about myself yet. Nevertheless, I thought a lot that evening about what she said about assuming people's conclusions. I decided not to think where these sessions would take me and to just let them happen. I was somehow hopeful that she would really help me to understand myself a little bit better.

The following morning, I woke up and repeated what was becoming a habit after only three days. I was at Karen's office just in time for the session.

"Hello Alvin. Come in, take a seat."

"Hi, thank you."

"Well, it seems congratulations are in order for both of us."

"How come?"

"Your third session. We are making a record here. I was not sure if you would come today."

"Well, here I am, so let's start."

"That is a very good attitude, Alvin. Yes, let's start. Why are you here?"

"Oh, come on. Not again."

"Ok, let's pause that question for a minute. What are you doing here, in Hobart? You don't live here according to your form. Is it work, holidays, or just these sessions? You could have gotten a therapist in Melbourne. There are plenty of them, and exceptionally good ones."

"It is not work, and it is not holidays. Holidays at the psychologist don't seem too much of a holiday to me. I have my reasons."

"I know you do. You don't do things randomly. In your head, there is a reason you chose Hobart. A very precise and thoughtful one. What is it?"

"You will think it is a silly one."

"Don't assume my thoughts, Alvin. We have been through that as well."

"I was in Iceland once. Looking for Sophie. Iceland is an island. Iceland it is just about as North as you can go looking for someone before hitting the North Pole. Tasmania is an island. Hobart is as South as I can go before going to the South Pole. In my head, I close a geographical variable."

"Alvin, I don't think it is silly. It suits you well. You try to close your variables like you would do in a project. However, honestly, I don't think anyone in this world would come up with something like that."

"Does that make me crazy?"

"Absolutely not. You are not crazy, that much I can tell. Yes, you have some issues you need to work out, but definitely not crazy. Let's talk about Sophie."

"Sophie? Right."

"You mentioned to me that you think about Sophie every day."

"That is right, every day. I mean, not in a compulsive obsessive way, but I do."

"So, what do you recall about Sophie when you think about her?"

"Sometimes, good memories or feelings between us, sometimes, the tough times and the split between us, sometimes. I wonder where she is and above all, how she is."

"Do you think she thinks about you every day?"

"I don't know. I cannot tell. I cannot answer that question. Maybe she does, maybe she doesn't. There is no way for me to tell."

"You have been in a relationship before, haven't you?"

"Yes, I have."

"But obviously you were able to move from those relationships. How did you manage before? Why is Sophie different?"

"Well, when I don't want something to bother me, I put it in a corner of my brain, and I just leave it there. I just ignore it. I am aware of it. I acknowledge it is there, but I choose not to bring those memories back. I am able to get closure on those feelings, and I am ok with that. Sophie touched me in a way no one had before, and I don't mean physically. She changed the way I looked at things, how I look at a picture, how I hear music, how I question life. Before I met Sophie, I thought I had a good grip on life, that I had some sort of control. After I met her, I realised that I knew nothing, or at least not as much as I thought I knew, and that I had yet way too many things to learn."

"Why didn't you get closure with Sophie? At the end of the day, you were the one leaving the relationship. It should be much easier for you to get closure than it is maybe for Sophie."

"True. I guess I just don't want to close that part of my life. I was not done learning with her."

"But you walked away from it anyhow."

"I did, but that doesn't mean I wanted to leave the relationship."

I think Karen noticed I was getting very uncomfortable answering those questions. It is not difficult for people to know when I am upset as I do nothing to hide it. Somehow, I was hoping for her to touch on another topic, but there wasn't really any other topic.

"Let me ask you something. Does it bother you, the thought of Sophie retaking her life with someone else, maybe having a family of her own, being happy?"

"No. No, it doesn't. To the contrary. I wish for her to be happy in any relationship she may decide to get in, or if she decides not to be in one, I wish her to be happy as well."

"Do you really mean that? Are you being honest on this?"

"110 per cent! I mean it, and I am being honest on this. I loved Sophie back then and I love her now. Why would I wish for her not to be happy? Makes no sense."

"She wanted to be happy with you, and you turned her down. Why?"

"It would not have worked."

"Alvin, see? You assumed. You assumed it was not going to work. You didn't know. No one knows until you live through it. Have you been in any other relationship since then?"

"No, I haven't."

"Have you tried it?"

"No, I haven't."

"Why?"

"I have lost faith in people, somehow. I lost faith in myself I guess. As I said, after I met Sophie, I was much more observant about what people do, how they behave, what they give, what they take."

"And what have you observed?"

"Everyone wants to win, no one wants to lose, and people are less and less likely to compromise."

"Would you care to elaborate on this?"

"I think we are being more and more selfish. We are unable to accept other people's shortcomings. We expect perfection and everyone gets upset when they don't get it. It doesn't matter, telling people you are not perfect.

They will say everything is ok, but the day you fail, they will get mad at you anyway. That creates issues, trauma, deception, you name it."

"So, why are you here?"

"Because I have a fucking void! A void! A void I am unable to fill or close. A void that every time it seems to close slightly my head reopens it. A void I don't want to close, because if I do, Sophie will be out of my life forever and I don't want that. Because I took a decision I really didn't want to take, and still, I did take it. Yes, I know I broke her heart and by doing so, I broke mine as well. I hurt someone I really loved, and I cannot get over it, that's why I am here!"

I am not a person who loses his temper easily, but I guess Karen had me where she wanted me to be. This sudden loss of manners caught her a little bit off guard. Talking loudly is not in my character.

"I...I apologise. I'm sorry, I lost my temper...I..."

"It is ok, Alvin. At least now we know why you are here."

"I'm sorry."

"Just breathe in and breathe out. Relax. It is ok. All that was in your head and now it is out. You are doing very well. I understand this is not easy for you at all. You are an engineer; you are used to solving problems. That's what you do. I understand it may be quite frustrating for you not being able to solve one. Relying on other people is never easy, but you need to accept the help and understand it is just another tool in your problem-solving. Look, it is almost time already. Why don't you take it easy the rest of the day? Try not to think too much in these last five minutes. Don't feel bad about it."

"Yes, I think I will. Tomorrow, same time?"

"Actually, I was wondering if you would like to have a day off and recover a bit."

"I had rather not. I need to finish this. I cannot stop now."

"You are walking a very fine line. It is better you take a day off."

I had rather not."

"You have waited for years; you can wait one more day. Take the day off. I'll see you in two days. Same time."

"Fine."

I left the building angry. Now I had another problem. What to do for another almost two full days in Hobart. The weather was still as bad as it could get. I decided to spend the rest of the day in a spa. I went through a cycle of massage, sauna, swimming pool, sauna, and massage again. At least my back and shoulders were loose. I went for a nice seafood dinner at a place in the harbour just in front of the hotel. I was the only person having dinner alone and that always made me somehow uncomfortable, so I finished my meal and went back to my room.

I slept well that night. I woke up relaxed with no stress of going back to my therapy. Maybe Karen knew best, and I was better off with a break. I got out of bed and opened the curtains for a beautiful, clear sunny day. The views were worth the extra money I was paying to stay at the ocean side of the building. I decided I was not going to stay indoors for the day. I opened my laptop, and I planned a small route. I packed my gear, got the car, and headed to Port Arthur.

I think I hit what every other tourist would do in that place. It is not something I would normally do, but I took all the guided tours through the various places in the area. I finished the day at a lookout facing south, thinking about all the places I had been during the last years, and how little I had enjoyed most of them. 25? 26 different countries? Most of them for work. I was always on the run and never had enough time to really explore them. At least, Australia would not be one of them.

On my drive back, I began to think about what would happen the following day at Karen's office. Karen really got me to talk about deep feelings and thoughts that I had. I have to give her credit for that, but again, that was her job. She should be good at it. She should be able to dig up all those feelings and thoughts, but I'm sure, as she said, I was not the easiest person to treat.

"Hello, Alvin, come in."

"Hi, Karen. Thanks."

"How are you, how do you feel?"

"Good, good. Thanks. You were right. A day off was the right direction."

"I'm glad it worked for you. Let's begin."

"Yes, ok."

"Tell me, are you a happy person, Alvin?"

"It is not an easy question to answer. I don't lack anything."

"Come on, Alvin, you know what I am trying to get to."

"I think people are happy when they feel complete."

"Are you complete?"

"No, you know I have a void. That's why I'm here, remember?"

"Yes, I do."

"Do you think if Sophie and you were together, you would be fully complete?"

"I hope not."

"That is an interesting answer, Alvin. What do you mean?"

"I know I have said that someone is happy when that someone is complete, but maybe I should have said 'almost complete'. Almost being complete is what pushes people to look for happiness, to progress somehow. If someone is almost happy, they will always strive for more. Completeness or happiness is an end road with no turning back and no exits."

"How much does this lack of completeness push you every day? How much does Sophie push you to do things every day even when she is not present in your life?"

"Sophie pushes my life every day. She still pushes me to do things. Interesting things, not the day-to-day stuff. She is the one pushing me to look at things in a unique way. Any creative thing I do beyond work is Sophie pushing me somehow to do it."

"Give me an example."

"Write. I write short stories. Actually, it is funny, because I hate to read, but I love writing."

"That is very odd. We should have a session just on that topic of not reading but writing. What do you write about?"

"I don't know. I write about thoughts I have, about feelings mostly. Playing with words somehow. Hiding messages, thoughts in words. That's what writing is about anyway, right?"

"Who reads your stories?"

"No one. Those stories are for me to write, not for others to read. I just write things."

"Do you read your own stories?"

"No, as I said, I don't like to read. I write everything on the go. I don't have a brainstorming session, handwritten notes or anything like that. I don't even proofread myself. I'm an engineer, not an artist."

"Don't you think an engineer can be an artist as well?"

"Oh, yes for sure they can be. Just not this engineer."

"Let's try a different topic. Tell me about the heists."

"The heists? What about them? I told you already. There were two of them, one in Munich, one in Bologna. After that, I decided that I could not do that anymore, and Sophie and I took different paths."

"Tell me. Did Sophie ever show what she got out of those heists?"

"No, she never did."

"Did you ask her?"

"Yes, I did."

"What was her answer?"

"That I was better off not seeing it so I could play innocent, in case things went south."

"Did you believe her?"

"Yes, I did. Why wouldn't I?"

"Alvin. Has it ever occurred to you that Sophie maybe never stole anything?"

"What do you mean? I drove her to those places. I waited in the car. I took the escape routes. I was there."

"Still, you never saw anything that she could have taken."

"No, they were small pieces of jewellery, she could have put them anywhere."

"Alvin, you just drove Sophie to a building and waited exactly ten minutes for her. Both times. How come it was exactly ten minutes? No one can be that precise. She had never been to Bologna before. How could she possibly have all the information for the heist?"

"She said she had contacts in the city."

"What if everything was a stage? A way to symbolise something? A way to test you? A game to play?"

"What the hell are you talking about? Are you telling me that nothing was real?"

"Let me find my notes. Hold on. Ok, here they are. Remember when you told Sophie that you couldn't do the heist anymore and you told her that mistakes could be made, implying also that the heists were a mistake?"

"Yes, I do."

"What did Sophie reply to you?"

"'You are not a mistake.'"

"'This not a mistake.' 'You are not a mistake.' What do you think it meant or it means?"

"I...I don't know."

"Alvin, do you think that she was just trying to tell you that stealing would be worth it if you were the reward? That's why the heists were perfect, and you would never be caught."

"No! That cannot be. It makes no sense. We were already together. Why play that game?"

"Completeness. You two are alike, think alike. Complex people mix with complex people. If completeness were a circle, she understood that she needed to have the circle opened somehow. Something that would keep the spark going. You both needed to keep looking. She needed that, and she understood you needed something as well. You told me before happiness is 'almost completeness'. Maybe Sophie understood that as well. I have to admit that the whole idea is a little farfetched, but in my head, it makes sense. Maybe by rejecting the heists you were rejecting the striving for happiness together that she was proposing."

"But why make this elaborate game? She was always very direct. She didn't like going around 20 times for the same thing."

"Alvin, you are an overly complex person to read."

"No, I am not.""Yes, you are. Alvin, after each of our one-hour sessions, I need another two hours on my own just to understand and process your thoughts as they are not straightforward. Behind your logic of ones and zeros, you process millions of calculations and thoughts and analyses. Sophie knew that. Maybe she was scared to be too direct with you. Alvin, where is Sophie now?"

"I don't know. I have been looking for her for years."

"Are you telling me that in the 21st century, you are unable to find a person? Alvin, you are not being honest now. Not with me, not with you. Why don't you contact her? Are you afraid?"

"...yes, I am."

"Why?"

"Because she will reject me. That nothing will be the same. Fear of failure. Fear of not being up to her and hurting her again.""Alvin. You do not know. You don't and there is only one way to solve your puzzle, which is giving her a chance. Give yourself a chance. But it is all up to you. You have to take that step."

"I don't think I have the courage for that."

"You found the courage to kiss her in that cafe in Munich."

"That was different."

"Why was it different?"

"I didn't have a plan. I didn't think. I just let go."

"Then, let it go! Alvin, let it go. That precise moment when you kissed her, it was that precise moment that you were yourself. Not an output of a deep thoughtful process. You need to let it go and be yourself, but no one can take that step but you."

"I know."

"Ok, time is up. I will see you tomorrow."

"I don't think that would be necessary. I think I got out of these sessions what I wanted. I am clear on what to do to almost close my void. Thank you."

"I understand, Alvin, and, yes, I think the progress you have made in the sessions is just wonderful. If you feel you are ready to move on, I wish you the best in your next steps. I have to say that you have been a challenging patient, and you have been up to the expectations I had when I took you in."

"Thank you."

"Before you go, and out of curiosity, when you stopped the other attempts at therapy, what was the conclusion you assumed that the psychologist would eventually get to?"

"That everything was up to me, to decide the next steps. But don't feel bad, you really have driven me through my feelings very well, and I truly appreciate your help."

"You are good at projecting things, still, don't assume and give chances. Good luck. Goodbye, Alvin."

"Goodbye, Karen."

Karen really had brought a lot of thinking into me. I don't think I had ever opened up to anyone in that way before. Definitely, she was good at her job. Now it was again all up to me.

I took my rental car and I drove to the places that bring me peace and time to reflect. The beach. There is this long beach close to Hobart airport called Seven Miles Beach. I parked my car in one of the parking areas and I began walking on the beach. This beach was a great spot for me as the plane landing's glide path was just above the beach. I sat on the sand looking at the ocean and listening to the waves breaking at the shore. A sound that was just interrupted by an aeroplane roaring as it went over my head.

"Hello, Alvin."

"Hi, what the hell are you doing here?"

"Remember that morning in Keflavik airport? I told you we would meet again. Here I am."

"I don't need you anymore. I told you then and I'm telling you now."

"I have always been in your head all the time, and you decided to bring me back just now."

"Go away, I don't need you."

"Don't worry. I will go but before I go, tell me, what are you going to do? Are you going to walk into the ocean or are you going to call her?"

"Don't make jokes with that. You know I have thought about walking into the ocean several times."

"I know you have"

"So, what are you going to do?"

"I don't have a plan."

"That is perfect, you work much better when you don't have one. Then, things will work out just fine."

I saw the next plane coming to land. I thought it was funny that I was in Seven Miles Beach, after being in seven airports, in seven years. I had no plan, and I wasn't sure what to do, just like Munich. I let the roar of the plane fade away and I picked up my phone.

"Hello, Sophie. Would you dare to go for a heist with me?"

Printed in the USA
CPSIA information can be obtained
at www.ICGtesting.com
CBHW070757280924
14967CB00089B/1056